RUINS, CHILD

Giada Scodellaro was born in Naples, Italy and raised in the Bronx, New York. Giada's writings have appeared in the *New Yorker*, *BOMB* and *Harper's Magazine*, among other publications. Her debut collection, *Some of Them Will Carry Me*, was named one of the *New Yorker*'s best books of 2022.

'Giada Scodellaro is one of the most astonishing writers of her generation and *Ruins, Child* is a visionary novel. Scodellaro refracts and redefines the canon of Black culture, the archive of Black experience. The result is a masterpiece that lives and breathes on the page, every sentence shimmering with wit, musicality, brilliance and verve.'
— Katie Kitamura, author of *Audition*

'Giada Scodellaro's newest masterpiece, *Ruins, Child*, endows the concept and form of the contemporary novel with new force and meaning. Cinematic and prismatic, like a camera constantly in motion and yet incisive in its close portraitures of a community of Black women and femmes surviving and living amidst the future urban, eco-dystopic, queer ruins of our society, Scodellaro's novel breaks new ground in spectacular fashion.'
— John Keene, author of *Counternarratives*

'*Ruins, Child* takes us to the crumbling architecture of a future past; a future past that is possibly now. In this work of fractal seeing, we encounter women in lives that are simultaneously lived, reenacted and observed. *Ruins, Child* is conceptually rich, prismatic and choral, embodied and surreal, cinematic and textual. Giada Scodellaro writes us Black life watching Black life.'
— Dionne Brand, author of *A Map to the Door of No Return*

'Scodellaro's brilliant prose breathes strangely. She captures and conjures a world and a set of characters so unlike anything I've ever encountered before, and there's a quiet terror furring beneath the story.'
— Mona Arshi, author of *Somebody Loves You*

Fitzcarraldo Editions

RUINS, CHILD

GIADA SCODELLARO

CONTENTS

PART I, *the film*

THE LEG, A LINE. [14]

THE LENS IS COVERED IN GREASE? [29]

THE DIVINITY OF NEON ORANGE. [44]

CHATTER. [48]

TEMPORARY FIXINGS. [53]

OLD ASS ARCHITECTURE. [58]

LATENESS. [60]

◆

PART II, *the text*

RIGHT THIGH / ON THE FOREARM /
SOLE OF THE FOOT / GROIN /
ON THE LACE OF TWO WRISTS 70

•

PART III, *the film continued*

AN UNCEREMONIOUS EXIT. 112

CHICKEN BONES. 113

THE COMMUNITY CENTER. 121

LANDSCAPING. 122

THE PLASTIC AND THE GUNS. 126

SUPRASTERNAL NOTCH/88DB. 136

PRICE OF ENTRY. 137

CLAY. 139

SHOULDERS. 142

LILIES TO SHREDS. 143

KNEES. 150

RUINSCHILD. 151

•

PART IV, *the sound*

TAPE 1 156

TAPE 2 159

TAPE 3 162

the woman who is over ninety
cries for her mother.   if our dead
were here they would save us.
— Lucille Clifton, 'dialysis'

PART I, *the film*

THE LEG, A LINE.

A close up of a woman's leg. And the leg is seen because the woman is tying her shoes.

Isn't the leg a line?, she's heard saying. Tying up the laces. There's a certain name the neighbors use when her leg sticks out of place. Out of place for a woman, you know. Out of place for how the body should be presented, even while tying a shoe. She hears voices from the front room. A little skin of the upper leg being shown outside of its intended context, that's when the neighbors take it upon themselves to call her out of her name.

She's fast, someone says in a low register, or it's just about the way her thighs push together when she bends, and her ass, her titties sitting.

Are we wrong to lament the condition of those structures?
—And aren't they ours?

In the footage the woman bends, loops her fingers around the laces, once, twice, grass stains on her knees. She stands, the people stare. Or she moves about, this figure, pushing the shopping cart and they all go at her pace.

The camera lens is covered in grease, we notice, there's an amateurish quality to all this. It's nighttime. The woman is lit up by the fluorescent lighting. She knows the store well, *the butter beans are over there*, she says, pointing.

The volume on the television is up loud. We follow her down aisle five. She checks the ingredients on the label, her long nails tapping the cans, later brushing her forearms against the fresh produce, the mustard greens. A swiping of a card, and they all pause for the sliding door. It is only when she's ready that they exit.

Lit up by streetlight; silver around the forehead.

We're sitting on the living room carpet watching the 168 hours of footage. The schools are closed up for the

Holiday. The footsteps of the children are heavy, running wild. We're watching the part of the film when the woman is running errands and the like. Our community mostly walks, and there was a time when this woman walked about: back from the market, to the gardens, barefoot from the lake, on the community center table, to the bridge, in the mud, dragging her soles (dirty) around the house—though now she is bedridden. Confined to bed, riding the bed.

We sit up in her house and watch her go still. We watch the footage, and watch her lead the others through the streets. It doesn't seem right how much the woman walks in the film, the ease of movement, arms swinging, not unlike a piece of metal, *the metal metal, metal of waiting,* the neighbor Dionne Brand says, or how often the woman remains on her feet.

She's carrying a purse on her shoulder, a faux-leather, black. Her purchases bagged up by a teen. She carries loads of mustard greens, prune juice, ginger ale, vaseline, butter beans.

And they shadow her. They gather around her, this elusive figure, *don't she move quick?* The six of them scale her. They move in unison. Do you know about that? About moving as a unit? It's harmonious. *Here come the six,* they used to say, *the six mix, here they are: the six fix, six peas in a pod, the six horsemen, the six kings-men*, the neighbors would say. *Here they come.*

And when the woman drops down to tie a shoe they wait for her to finish. And the audience waits, in the living room the children quiet down their games. They check their own little shoes to see if they need tending.

Her thigh is out of place and shiny with oils. She's gotten the necessary things—the turkey neck, the cowpeas, white vinegar.

The volume is raised up too high, *It must be explained*, the woman says, yells, profile to the camera, thighs sticking, strawberry skin, razor bumps showing, the mini skirt, climbing, tattoo peeking, walking slow, and all of them walking side by side—*it must be explained how the Hill is raised but almost flat, not at all hilly*, she says, mouth wide, *and it sits on a salt marsh that is known to be sinking. Named after a certain somebody, a politician or something, a something something Hill*, the woman says. *Do you know about this place?*

The group speeds up their walking to keep time with her. *Yes*, one of them says. *Perhaps it was an Augustus Troy Hill or a Jamaal Amenite Hill, we don't really know.*

The woman is beginning to forget, to misplace things, and the others, the six, they let her tell them again, again, *A something something Hill*, though they know this speech. On her feet: tennis shoes.

The valley is familiar, it is the same now as it was then, during the taping, and before. So we've known it and the surrounding flatness for many years, decades. It is sinking a little, but then everything is going down, so today we tell ourselves *it is fine*, and just the same there is the Holiday, or there is an urge to preserve something. *This film, it's about place, community*, she says, *being rooted in the Hill, the way we are rooted, okay, and it's about our Holiday or about tradition, and your place here—you.*

Okay, they say. *Okay, okay.*

The group never uses the word unless there is something silly going on. *To sit in the grasses, to talk to the neighbors, to excavate*, the woman tells the six. *Okay*, they repeat. They walk on. They walk behind the gigantic head of this woman, this too tall woman. *And get my good side*, she says. She towers over them like a pine. There are hills in the distance, and the fog is down low. The camera captures this. Her pace does not give her age away. The woman is old, and she is with child.

It is what it is, the woman says, or *the name has stuck.*
The name?
Yes, honey, the name, The Hill.

The geese, which are aggressive and almost completely gone, stomp when they are near, demanding something. The six, *the six hits*. And they do film the animals, the birds, and are somewhat distracted by them, even though they are not the focus of the project.

And the woman says, *film the ducks, film the geese, oh yeah. Capture something good, the ducks are full of good.*

We sit on the living room floor, on the sixteenth floor, watching the footage. Do you get it? The wide shot of the buildings, how they exist on the very end of the salt marsh, the artificial lake, the high school, the market, the cemetery, the hospital, the thick asphalt. Asphalt so thick and suspended that we all have difficulty climbing across the street, this whole place is cool to the touch. The prison sits empty.

It is a tradition to watch it, you understand, and the thing is so long that most of us have only seen bits and pieces. The movie is all out of order. *I have seen it all, memorized it. Would I not know a thing that covers?*

Those who are tired get up to leave. The neighbors are off to church or going straight to their bed, to praise or to rest, respectively, and the film is forever playing in the background.

Leaving and returning, taking turns. This will go on for a week or so. The woman with her bare feet in the soil, sitting on a stoop or in the grass. The woman on her knees. The six are swarming around her. Sometimes it is quiet and still. Moss, the grasses, which are dry and yellow, weeds, weeds. Yellow, or golden, like wood can be golden. And furniture being cut from pine, molded, sewed, finished. The pine trees swaying.

And the woman's name is Vonetta!.

Vonetta!, though the neighbors call her something else entirely (*fast!*), and we mostly refer to her as she exists (*the woman!*). *Oh, but I don't like to be reduced.*

It's Vonetta!, she says when she introduces herself to any man or woman, or child. *With an exclamation point at the end*, the woman continues, an aircraft moving past.

Some stragglers have joined, they adjust themselves on the carpeted floor, finding a free space, or a gap, the arm of the plastic couch. They sit up straight to watch this thirty year old film. *Vonetta!, this is how the name is written on the birth certificate, I can show it to you, though it might fall apart a little more in our hands, yellowed.*

Vonetta!, the woman explains, *is the name given by my mother to prepare me for how I would be called out, or how I would be erected, enacted, blamed. The punctuation at the end like a nail left in a wall.*

Sometimes in the living room we fall asleep.

When we wake the children are gone, maybe to school, and the apartment is otherwise packed with new faces.

The gals (6) as they stand on the corner waiting for the bus to pass. And the street is paved with asphalt so thick that the sidewalks are not aligned with it. They (6) wear clothes that reflect the decade. Someone beating a carpet from an open window just out of frame while we beat the carpet from the next window. Just behind—the Hutchinson River/the Hutchinson River. There is some repetition going on. How to explain it? Everything we did once, we still do.

There are some preparations going on that have always been going on: the lights being arranged upon the branches of the sweetgum. We are all squished inside the apartment, preparing, watching/waiting for a glimpse of ourselves.

Climb up, the bus driver, Charlie, says.

Charlie is dead. He is captured in the scene as we remember him: eyebrows touching, goatee, low sideburns, waves, hair connecting over his surfaces. There's so much traffic. To get on a bus is to spend some time climbing aboard, or being pushed from behind, or being pulled up by the armpit.

Climb on sweetie pie, the bus driver calls out to the six.

Bitch, the bus driver calls out.

Fuck you Charlie, they say, one at a time. They climb up one at a time. They help the woman climb up easy. She is careful to show the thigh. *There is something graceful about the gesture*, a child comments. More chatting, the camera turns away to shoot some B-roll. The six voices harmonize. They go around the loop, *Einstein Loop*. The bus is clean. Things moving fast outside, and they watch the lights coil in the red maple, and the milk thistle leaning over or resting.

We are losing interest. *Milk thistle is good for the liver disease*. The sky is grey. We move to the kitchen to watch the others play spades. *Isn't this her floor, her ground?*

Windows open, we sit upon chairs upholstered in green materials. It is hot as hell. On the television the earth is frozen solid. *Camera is heavy, hell*, they take turns resting the equipment upon different shoulders, a muffled sound, *The earth is frozen solid*, they say in unison. The picture is shaky, with the image pointing all the way up—hands turned solid.

The students are gathering their books. The woman reaches into her left sock to pull out some cash. She flashes it to the camera. A high pitched giggle, contagious, low and too loud. Her breasts shake.

The six tell the woman to shush/hush.

When she is done fucking around, bragging, she pushes the money into her bosom. The woman is performing. *It takes courage to be calm*, she says, stepping off the bus. *Y'all seem nervous, nervous to make a fuss and I'm as calm as a cucumber.*

We're not nervous, one says, maybe Pearl, *we're tired.*

The dimensions of the buildings are even, with the exception of the one building in which most of us still live, Number 35, the tallest. And even in their weight these buildings are even, equal configurations in their overall size and width, with pillars that were built for the floods or for the quakes. The apartments are almost exactly uniform in their square footage, in their coloring, and in their overall demeanor. This is how it is, and how it will be.

The buildings are not to be fooled with, a neighbor, one of the six, Sanaa Lathan, says, having climbed off the bus after the woman. Six joints climbing across the street. Vonetta! mumbling something inaudible. Coughing into the crook of her elbow. The pregnancy is far along—the woman holds the curve. They take their time with her, they offer their twelve arms. Some of this effort is picked up by the lavaliere mic—

There are no new buildings sprouting up in the distance. There is no construction happening, none, and the city is done. No cranes. Everything is where it is meant to be, the woman says as they move toward the entrance of building Number 35, 30 keys shuffling in hand, 40?

Sanaa Lathan is trailing the group, Jackie comes up second. Then Seret, Mona. Beryl. Pearl. *All the things have already been built. Some of the pieces tend to fall off but they mostly remain in their place, okay*, the woman says.

The government repeats, Sanaa Lathan says, *they tell us*

over and over again, 'Let the pieces fall if they must'. Well, this shit is right falling apart, you understand?—before the woman, Vonetta!, responds, overlapping—*no more federal money will be invested into our buildings, or into their upkeep, mmmm, the infrastructure is in shambles—goddamn,* Sanaa Lathan cuts in—*goddamn.*

They talk over each other, the two women, Sanaa Lathan and this old ass woman, our woman—*of course, there are those that still wash the hallway floors, or glue the pieces of gravel back together.* They catch each other's eye.

Look at the white shoes, look at the white shoes!, they laugh, necks broken, a cambré, one arm elevated, laughing and arching to the high heavens. Sanaa Lathan has the last word, *Lord have mercy.*

Sanaa Lathan has a habit of interrupting. She wants things to go her way, or she hopes to impart some knowledge, or to make people see where she is coming from. *Do you see where I'm coming from?,* she says, *you understand?* She wants to be understood. She's forceful, imposing, overbearing in her communication. She's touchy feely.

A hand on the shoulder or on the hob of the knee. An elbow pushing out. She reaches for hands, she pats people on the back, pokes and squats down to pick people up off the dirty floor. *All in our faces,* the children say. Sanaa Lathan cradles some to her bosom. She bathes twice a day. It is not an exact thing, she's a contrarian, every popular idea is hers to contradict. She's lazy, and her shape was fine, is still fine. There is no difference between her then, her hips, and now, only the rheumatoid arthritis.

And we don't mind the way Sanaa is, Charlie says, *we'll gladly sit in her company.*

Other times we hear her humming something about gluing the pieces back together, a tune about the gravel, *pick up the pieces,* she hums/sings/scats. And when they are together (the woman and Sanaa Lathan)—they are like buffalo grass and bison, oil and vinegar. Don't they disagree about how to care for the gardens, the resurrection fern, or how to patch their garments with the sewing machine, how to grind the milk thistle down, how much turmeric and honey to put in, what kind of stitch to use, how many chairs to pull up to the function?

We didn't mind, *we don't mind their fussing, we let them be.*

Watching the woman making her way upstairs, off the elevator, into her domestic space, camera on her heels, and the apartment looks as it does now. *Pat is in the upper room*, Vonetta! says, *and I owe the man $350 in maintenance fees.* The space is the same, the furniture. *Don't lean against the china cabinet.*

The six horsemen follow upstairs, to the upper floors, into the apartment. They put the purchased items away. They begin to tidy up. The groceries have their place: the nonperishables on the high shelf, the produce washed with baking soda and put on paper towels to dry. It is practiced, a thing of nature. *The house smells of elderflower*, Beryl says—*no, you're wrong*, Sanaa Lathan says, *it smells of ginger leaf.*

Picture this: Vonetta! washing the hallway floors, Sanaa Lathan climbing on the couch to take a nap, Mona wiping down the counters, Jackie cutting the vegetables into cubes. Pearl dusting the piano.

The woman is old, I hear the children saying, their bodies warm against our hips, *not the way all adults are old, but really old, ancient, she is endless—*

The high cheek bones, we focus again on the cinematic thing, we attend to the six, split diopter, we listen to them performing their duties, and the way they speak on their ailing bodies: *put some peroxide on it*, Jackie says. Mona says, *rub her down with alcohol, then some Vicks, put the kettle on for the hot water bottle.* Pearl says, *soak in the tub with epsom salt.*

The woman is not slow in her movements, she is methodical. Her knees crack when she bends, something about collagen. She's swift, the way she moves the mop back and forth.

Youth fails us, the woman says. *Or when it moves away, this youthfulness, does it not subvert all expectation? Is all the good faith we had in ourselves, in our younger selves, all those expectations of grace coming along with this movement, was it all for naught? Where is the grace?*

Put some tea tree oil on it, some castor oil for the liver, Seret says.

The neighbors have always covered their domestic possessions with textiles, material to help maintain things, or to help their shit not fall apart. This is the reason for the shag carpeting, the plastic coverings. Everyone is afraid for things to become elastic.

Looseness—that is the thing people fear, in a person, in women, and in objects, we hear the woman saying, eyes closed, legs set wide on the plastic couch.

The seasons are thus: tropical or freezing. The seasons are such that the plants die and bloom in quick succession. *The things in between, this mildness, is short lived,* Jackie says. The leaves are there and they burn up quick, or they're under ice. Jackie is buried under the ice, but when she was around, awake, she liked to wink and to exaggerate things, she liked to discuss the weather, she could predict a rainfall like no other, *and it does feel sometimes*, Jackie used to say, *like the seasons are toying with us.* Jackie made lots and lots of money predicting the weather, erecting things, or playing the numbers. Her bob shaking while she talked, swinging; a third carpet being swatted from a window. Jackie lost money on the horses.

The woman is mopping the hall, the front door sits open.

And there are but two and a half seasons, no more, no less. Or it feels like it anyway, so there are two and a half alternating moods, no more, no less. I'm always hot as hell or freezing, Jackie says.

Not many are bothered by these temperature shifts. Clothing isn't made to express a thing, but to allow for cover or better circulation. The major Holiday is celebrated in frigid or humid temperatures, depending.

Landscape designs withstand for days, weeks, sometimes for many years and then the plants die or dry or are overridden.

Don't let the woman start up again, one of the neighbors says. *The grasses are too high.*

We call her fast thing, or Von or Vonetta!. We call her the woman. As if she is the only woman, the mother—*Wasn't she the mother?*, the children whisper to the screen.

Yes, the six say in unison, *the grasses are too high, the flora will withstand very little.*

From the window in the backroom, this high up, the view consists of this: people walking in a syncopated way, all over and small like ants, surrounded by the remnants of an evolving architecture of plant life. Water lilies, lime trees, hedges.

The day after next the basement is certain to fill up with water from the lake, it's gonna rain bad, Jackie says.

The volume of the television is up so loud it can be heard crystal clear in the backroom. *Mhmmm*, they say, *yes*, they say. *It's known that no basement apartment can really withstand or exist anymore, not like when I was a young thing, not even a first floor spot, or they exist, but they're occupied illegally, the government tells us, okay, and everyone that can manage lives up high*, the woman says.

And then Pearl asks her, *Von, Vonny, can plants be architecture? Can they exist in reverence the way the old castles still stand, broken? Or when we plant the cypress trees in a line, don't they provide good shade?*

The woman says *yes, yes. Sure.* Sanaa Lathan says, *no.*

The woman insists, *plants can be structural, and they are, but the more the landscape is lost to the aggressive seasonality the more their consistency is lost. Oh, but the cypress trees are as straight as a ruler, companions for the teenagers on their walks to school... do you ever pay attention to the cypress?*, the woman raises her voice, *you never pay it no mind, Lathan*—outside: lines, pearls, suddenly snow.

When it is permitted by weather, Sanaa Lathan interrupts, *the county produces vibrant foliage, real vibrant—the fauna and the flora, you know, the weeds, thistle, grasses, mosses and the fungi, delphinium, cacti (which last in the most uncomfortable of temperatures). Also those orchids, sunflowers, ribwort plantain...*

Or, the woman chimes in, *there is plant death all over, okay, ice. An absence is forged during this vegetal unmooring, can't you see how time or temperature can undo the landscape? Spoil it rotten?*

And the seasons are such that the plants die and bloom in quick succession.

The woman turns, she takes a break from mopping up the hallway, body squared and facing the camera, belly full, lines all over the forehead—*blooming and dying repeatedly. And though there is no end to this, none at all, and though the decay sets forth more growth, it is still striking to see something bloom over and over, okay, or for it to die in this quick succession, and for me this change is a swelling, a harmony, Lathan, it's divine!*

Everyone thinks it's divine. Sanaa Lathan does not wait for the woman to quiet, *Net, you think it's a gift from on high, and I don't want to blaspheme but the plants can be seen from anywhere you look, from the second floor of the community center, from this here window, from any manmade structure: life/death. It just is. From this height, up on the sixteenth floor, we know the transition. Don't we look down upon it every day? It's ours, you understand, it belongs to the mortals. And Pearl, you ask again and again, 'can plants be architecture? Can they exist in reverence the way the old castles still stand, broken?' You ask this of us over and over and over, when you know it's ours!*

There is mopping, dusting, cutting, resting going on. Someone coughing into their arm, a second train passing underneath. And the woman waits a while before she offers a conclusion: *plants are better than any buildings might be, better because the buildings split or lean pathetically, okay, and though the plants split and lean too, they are eager to find the sun.*

When the woman talks, she says, *okay, okay*, making sure they're keeping up with her. The group never uses the word unless there is something silly going on, *okay*, and when the woman uses it, they can't take her seriously.

Sanaa Lathan says, *do you know where I'm coming from?*, and the woman says, *okay, okay*. Jackie concludes her thought with a nod, a smile, and a wink. Pearl rolls her eyes. Mona sucks her teeth. Seret is quiet quiet quiet. The woman, she is quiet unless spoken to, and when spoken to is long-winded. She scratches her nose every few minutes, a tic, or she rubs her hands together, like so, or she plays with her scalp, sometimes drawing blood, scratching, patting it down. Beryl curses up a storm.

The woman calls Sanaa Lathan, Lathan. Sanaa Lathan calls the woman Net.

It isn't that the six don't have high reverence or respect for the woman—*no*—in fact, she is a pillar of the community. She has taught the group many things, many many things: for example, how to spit when frustrated, how to curse in a soft way, how to cure garlic and bundle it into groups of ten, how to fell trees, how to quit a job.

They sit with her in the backroom, still, to ask for advice/remedies. Though she is nonverbal, frozen, they go and they sit with her, they talk, asking her things, demanding help, or otherwise staying real quiet waiting, for some of her time/attention/gaze. They sit very close to the bed, very close to her, thinking of a question or visualizing the ask, and sometimes it is answered: a millipede on the wall, a crack on the ceiling, an object by the window moving to the floor, the wind.

She is always teaching, she never gets no rest, a child says, and in the next frame the woman can be heard saying: *chew up some tobacco, the snuff, place it on the open wound, and for the bee stings gather up those spider webs there, or some urine, rub it in and over.*

Looseness, that's the fear, and though she is the center of this place, though the woman is a direct descendant of the founders of this place, and therefore of the soil itself, and these old ass trees, and though her presence demands a certain level of regard, she is still considered fast, reckless, too generous, loose.

*An untended woman, untended to—*Beryl says, *an untended garden can still bring the neighbors to tears or bring us down to our fucking knees (depending on the skill of the landscape designer), and it is especially upsetting when the people of the Hill, our people, stumble upon the goddamn plants still in bloom while out for a short walk, or a thigh/trunk left uncovered. And then, on our way back home from the market, walking down a familiar path, walking straight down Gun Hill, on Burke, 233rd, 219th, Laconia, Olinville, Eastchester Rd., or wherever, the plants (thriving just an hour or two* *before) are no longer in bloom. Imagine it! Shit, and on these short walks when we encounter this woman, yes, you Von!, and your goddamn landscape designs (with our shopping bags in tow or our children in tow, butter beans in tow) going down near the lake, near the library and the high school, behind the market, we see you—untended to, free—and that's when we're most overcome, moved to tears or brought down to our ashy knees.*

THE LENS IS COVERED IN GREASE?

There is art in the apartment windows. Oh hell, the windows are covered with it: taped up with construction paper or with instructions for assembling furniture. During the Holiday most windows are covered with family photographs. The sun filters in low.

A photo of someone eating cake with her man, her man fitted in a black suit. White lace, a wedding.

The lens is covered. The lens is covered in grease from the rose shea butter offered to the crew by the woman. *I can't stand the look of some dry hands.* She rubs her hands together, moisturizing them, sitting down in the wooden chair to get the elbows, knees, the heel of the foot.

Some time has passed. The clothes are different, and the hair. A kettle is humming on the stove. Mona is unpacking, she yawns and her teeth are small in her mouth, *what a long neck*. The sound of garbage trucks going past, the oak trees turning. Below: an allée.

The women (6) are gathered around the television. We (107) watch them watching something. They eat dates. *We've seen this film so many times*, they say. They watch a version of the same film we are watching, but a shorter cut, an older version. The six getting up on the bus. We've seen them see this part so many times.

They talk about the landscape, they take turns reciting a word, *the landscape is thus*, they say: *weeds, blurry weeds. Buildings, birds*, and behind them someone is yelling; *goddamn*, or *what in the world, lord, lordy*, or *baby, where do you think you're going, dressed like that?* More sounds layered over these, over us—a car horn; a voiceover telling us that the garbage is turning around and around in the white garbage truck.

The garbage is turning around and around in a white

garbage truck, so loud, and that car engine revving up, Vonetta!'s voice says, a good voice, raspy, we hear it and the children repeat, *baby, baby, where the hell you think you're going, dressed up like that?*

It's Vonetta!, with an exclamation point at the end, yes, the woman repeats, and they adjust themselves, they sit up straight. An aircraft moving past, a 747. *Vonetta!, this is how the name is written on the birth certificate, though it is old and falls apart a little in our hands, yellowed/ruined. Vonetta!,* the woman explains, *the name was given to me by my father to prepare me for how I would be erected, called on to lead, heralded!*

A piece of art is missing from its place on the living room wall. I don't know what they've done with it, Faith Ringgold's *Church Picnic.* "Freedom Baptist Church Annual Sunday School Picnic," it reads. *Vonetta!, Vonetta!,* she is blurry from the shea butter.

Can we get a paper towel, or something to wipe the lens down? And the leg is seen because Vonetta! is bending over, getting ready to tie her shoe, a brushed leather.

She has a fine pair of legs.

A kick from the child, the skin near the bellybutton distended. The laces are always coming undone. *Isn't the leg a line?* Tying the laces. A little skin of the upper leg, *and soon,* the narrator tells us, Vonetta! tells us, *the temperature will reach 37 degrees Celsius.*

The lens is wiped clean. Vonetta! is at the window and at first it's this: the mountains behind her, the building where she has remained all of her life (except for a week's time) and where her parents once lived, the great-grandparents, all of her people, her aunts, a five room apartment. She stands like this, and the women (6) are always a hand's throw away, then she turns, blurry, and she is cut in half, off-center, we take in half of her back, half of her backside.

This goes on for three hours or so. Sanaa Lathan is downstairs, refusing to watch, refusing to see herself watching her young self onscreen, and refusing, thus, to participate in tradition.

Sanaa Lathan downstairs, in front of the building. Her shape giving her away, it's the same, the same. She's standing in front of some poplar trees; and in the right bottom corner of the frame there she is again, younger, quicker, the same, among the six and among the old poplars. Two of her. One on the old television, another downstairs. From the window we see Sanaa Lathan moving with imprecision, sloppy, she's sitting on a bench, drinking from a flask, talking to anyone moving past. Her head is rolling, she's laughing, talking, chatting, arguing. Vonetta! gets up, walks past the living room window. Sanaa is beckoning the neighbors to her. Vonetta! is picking things up, tidying, collapsing cardboard boxes, approaching the window, unpacking bit by bit. The wind moves the leaves of the poplar, an empty train calling out, though we know it will not stop, it moves past.

The sound of Mona's legs moving back and forth on the couch. Vonetta! takes a break, she sits near Mona on the plastic couch. Mo, we call her. Mo's legs moving up and down, jumping. Vonetta!'s legs and Mona's legs are different, we notice, and we have all argued over whose legs are most effective, or most attractive.

Mona is humming something, sitting on the couch and her calves are underdeveloped. She smokes a cigarette. Silver ring on the index finger. A diamond ring on the ring finger. Mo's engaged to be married. There it is: Vonetta!'s set of muscular thighs set against the jumping of Mona's skinny calves, and the back of Mona's left hand is now right on top of Von's forehead. Checking to see if she has a temperature. *She had a temperature yesterday,* Mona tells the camera. Someone reminds her not to fill them in, maybe Jackie, *just exist, speak as you always do or address us only if we ask something specific.*

Mo rolls her eyes all the way up and around. She kisses her teeth. Mona's hands are on Von's forehead, fingernails looking a mess. There's music playing, a score from a film. A saxophone? Or a bassoon in the background, a car horn blaring. The horn, and the record player is familiar to us. Vonetta! is sweaty and warm to the touch.

Someone, maybe Jackie, asks Mona if she worries for Vonetta! or if she has taken on the role of caretaker, *do you worry Mo? Do you play the role?,* she doesn't respond, she ignores them.

Vonetta! pulls out a photo album, hundreds of family photos.

Well, that's daddy. We called him Obit, in his suit. And look at me, this is me when I was a young thing, okay?—

Did y'all hear, Mona interrupts, *about the thing happened over at the school? How someone set half the building on fire? How everyone rushed down there and then the fighting began? How the water ran down the sidewalk from the hose and the hydrant and how that one girl was blamed what's her name? Matches yes she's being blamed simply because of her name she's catching all the heat catching hell but she denies it. And wouldn't it be something a girl named Matches if she had committed the crime the arson though we don't believe she had anything to do with it not at all. And all the files got burned up all the records. And then there was another fire the next day and the day after. Three fires! The girl was blamed for those too but she wasn't even in town. She denies it vehemently and Matches couldn't have done it no way her people had already sent her south she's gone. But now the government is calling for her to pay to apologize or to finance some kind of rebuilding effort they want to send Matches the fine in the mail even though she hasn't done a thing she's innocent... now we've heard it's unfortunate just today we heard how the girl Matches she has burned something down after all a prophecy fulfilled isn't it funny her grandmama's house down south burnt to the ground an accident of course we know started while playing with a lighter or while trying to warm her fingertips.*

Mona undresses. They continue filming and she consents. *I don't give a damn about a camera*, she says, *who's gonna see this outside of us?*

Mona's breasts are exposed.

It is not sexual, she's just removing a white shirt, a bra, changing into another shirt—and she is with her people, breasts hanging, her girlfriends—a polo, a sort of uniform.

Mona sits back on the couch. Vonetta!'s calves not moving at all, and her arms are raised high as she unpacks an alarm clock from cardboard. And the filmmakers (Jackie/Beryl/Seret) would say things, like *we'll overlay a branch from one of the poplar trees upon Mona's breasts (medium) in post-production.*

The branch getting pushed around by the wind downstairs while Vonetta! gets up and puts on the kettle. Mona sits down again, legs jumping. So there are layers to this: see one set of breasts and a poplar tree, the sound of plastic, Sanaa Lathan on the bench out front, the director(s) using natural light to get the shot.

Everything is tiny on the television within the television, watching the women as they sit very still, watching Vonetta! unpack some books: *To Be Young, Gifted and Black; Dust Tracks On the Road; Chosen Poems, Old and New; 'Fore Day Mornings: Poems*—and we are lost in the potential of this scene, and in the bodies of these two heifers, their chest cavities, even if we understand that they're all just going about their mundane business.

The bosom is just the fruit, a child whispers, *though it is true that there are those who will make a fuss over a breast.*

As an audience we convince ourselves that when a breast is shown onscreen it is meant to unmoor, or to provide nostalgia. *This is meant to unmoor*, we say. *Misogyny allows for this*, but Mona doesn't mind, she accepts the extra cash offered to her, $250.

Vonetta! offers to expose her breasts too (small), *what for that fee, you can see these hills too*, she says, laughing. *Who's funding this?*, and she unclasps her bra with one hand. *The branch from a paper birch tree will be overlaid upon Vonetta!'s modest bosom*, the director says. She flashes her modest bosom, and the branch from a paper birch tree is overlaid upon them.

We have just returned to the Hill, Mo says, *we were gone for a week, after a failed attempt at moving to a new place, moving west or somewhere altogether new.*

We are not wholly afraid of the nudity, the director starts up again, maybe Jackie, *that is not why we cover the nipples with a poplar branch and with a paper birch trunk. It's quite the opposite, we want to know you and we want to make art!*

The audience laughs at this.

The branch moves in the wind downstairs, below the window.

The breast is not the focus, the directors explain as they hand over the crisp paper bills. *It's just a vessel.* Later they turn their attention to the feet, an abrupt shift, ten minutes of feet, and though the heel of the foot is somewhat cracked, the toes are taken care of, shaped, clean, and painted in a metallic bronze.

When the breasts are finally set aside, and the shirts pushed back down over their heads, the perspective moves to a bird's-eye view of the two separate scalps, a split screen, using a ladder and some tape they set the camera up from the ceiling. Mona's scalp versus Vonetta!'s, the hair parted into thirty-six boxes or into two plaits, respectively, and there's one belly that protrudes, in utero, and the other that is empty and somewhat flat, and these two women are finally imagined from above. It is here that Vonetta! says to Mona,

hell, I don't feel so well.
You don't feel well?
No, not at all.
You don't have a temperature.
No.
No.
But I'm feeling very lousy and hot, very warm, my shirt is almost all the way soaked through, (cough), and I'm sleepy, so damn tired, lethargic, and the circulation in my leg is off, way off, and every time I stand up it hurts or tingles. It hurts to go up the stairs. My feet hurt like hell.
Yeah, you feel clammy... clammy as shit, and after all the contractions it makes some kind of sense. But you don't have a temperature.
I know... and the neighbors are talking again.
Yeah?
Yeah.
That's what they do. What about?
That's all they do, God bless them. Never minding their business that pays them. Talking about how Jackson is broke how he spent all his wife's hard earned money gambled it away or how money is running low the social security fund is running low or about Lathan's acting how they didn't like it much and they didn't like the man playing opposite her or about the child this the child that when is he coming?, they ask. And they don't know he's already come... and about how everyone should get an air purifier.
Should we get one?

Maybe.
Yes.
And then we can bring it with us when we go again.
Yes.
Pack it right along with us.
Yes.

When Vonetta! begins to cry, to sob, Mona says, *Oh, baby, I bought you lemons. Lemons, and honey. The tea you like ginger tea bottled water. Water sealed in glass. The tap water's no good I keep telling you. And I bought you a new vibrator and some crusty bread. That soft cheese you like. Peach jam. Ginger root.*

And then Von says to Mona, and to the camera too, still hanging from above, she looks at the ceiling, tears rolling down and puddling on the carpet, she looks up when she says it, *that's good, that's good.*

The trees are blowing, not just this poplar. We don't understand the why of the trees, why they still exist in this godforsaken place. *Who planted these nonnative species in the Hill?*

And the audience doesn't really understand much of what is going on. The editing is chaotic. Though we do know how the trees were used for violence/are still used, *we do know what Alice Coltrane was plucking her fingers raw about, goddamn*, a child says.

The trees are getting blown to bits.

So the woman gets up, she moves the ladder to the corner. She tidies up, she walks toward the backroom, we don't move with her. Vonetta! walks with both hands behind her back, hands clasped. Or with one hand on her hip, one on her belly. When she makes her way down the hall she takes one hand from the belly or from the hip, places it on the wall, and drags it along, the drips from a bad paint job pushing under her fingers.

From the backroom she gives a play-by-play: *I'm removing my shirt, replacing it with a clean one real slow-like because my back is killing me my lower back is really killing me*, she says, *it's the arthritis or the fibromyalgia or the pre-diabetes.* She doesn't wear a bra, *what is the point, at my big age?*, and for a moment her square nipple is exposed while she yells out, *my nipple is out you want to come throw more money at me?* No one takes offense.

The crew is crowded into the hallway.

Mona is moaning about something or another, squeezing through the bodies in the hall, stomping and heavy-footed, squeezing behind to get to the bathroom, *I'm late for work*, she says.

The woman's wooden dresser is long and sits low. The wood is dark. Nothing on the walls, nothing on the dresser except a ceramic vase and a coconut palm plant. On the floor, a mirror.

What is almost missed if you're not paying attention (if you're facing the wall or if you're focused on the goings on of the superimposed trees, the white pine, the neighbors yelling out, or the shower turning on, or even on Vonetta!'s detailed account of her state of dress/undress) is a faint knock at the front door, *tap tap tap*.

Mona is running out of the shower, slipping, wet, *tap tap*, squeezing past the crew, rummaging in the small kitchen, rumbling, frantic, grabbing a knife, unlocking the multiple locks of the front door, slipping off the chain lock while wrapped in a white towel, opening it—receiving a mango from a man, skinning it right there on the spot.

The tree flutters outside and below but we are ridiculous and looking at the wall, filming the wall, chatting about how it needs washing down, it needs repainting.

There is some commotion at the front door, a whispering. We hear a man call out, *Mooooooona*.

It goes on for a minute, two, three, and the woman in the backroom is uncovering and then covering up again. Taking off a clean shirt, deciding on another purchased from the merchant stands at the Velvet Rope tour. A man calling out from the front and the woman is pulling some pants up over her thighs, jumping, and unfortunately we're not paying attention to poor Mona, Mo, the camera faces a wall in the hallway and Vonetta! is not done dressing.

Vonetta! does know that man, the children say. His voice as he enters the space, his shoulders, he's a well known figure, and even though Mona is licking mango juice from her fingers, peeling the green skin back and chomping down on the fruit, this action is omitted, it's not captured, we are forced to imagine it—the mango Mona has just received from Burle.

We hear his voice, a tenor—*and did you hear about the thing happened down at the school? How that teacher set half the school on fire? Some think it was an accident but I know it wasn't no accident. How everyone rushed down there I rushed down there too and saw with my own two eyes yeah and then someone pushed me from behind and we started to tussle... how the water ran down the sidewalk puddles of water moving over our tennis shoes boom boom boom water going right down my socks and how that one girl was blamed... Matches Matches her real name is Margaret Little Margie didn't she almost burn down her grandmama's house? We heard the sound... three or four were hurt but it had nothing to do with the fire itself they were hurt before the fire even started because the building wasn't up to code! And when I fell down my back got all wet. Charlie beat my ass good. Look at this... and the fire department never came never and then they didn't come for the other fire either and another, and the one after that sure didn't lateness... a fire at the supermarket, the church set on fire...*

And the way Mona sucks on the mango Burle's brought over specifically for her is not suggestive, with the teeth biting or pulling, some juice splashing her eyeglasses (the large brown frames) and the way she is sucking and talking to Burle between bites, *good old Burle*, the liquid running down her knuckles, down her chin, peeling the green/orange skin of the bounty all the way back, arching her back, the act becomes like an inversion or a latching on.

Jackie is aware of the pair (Mona/Burle), though when she turns to capture them it is late. Vonetta! is aware too, all the way in the backroom, she knows, and now she's hurrying to put on the perfume, two fingers pressing into the skin of the wrists and behind both ears (rose petal and saffron) putting on some jewelry and her cold cream. Burle with his short chicken legs crossed one over the other and Mona is eating the hell out of a mango, calves jumping.

The pair begins watching a film together, though Mona is already late for work, *hasn't she told us so?*, a child says. It's just the way a mango must be consumed, we decide, at a pace and in a way that drips. *Audre Lorde eats a mango like that, as do some others*, a child says.

What they are watching from the plastic couch (that also pulls out into Mona's bed) looks something like a recording of three individuals, or a moment in the life of three fools stranded out at sea. We don't know which sea, it is blue. We cannot make out much, this third film, within the film, within a film. It could be a swimming pool, a lake. The third television is puny.

The stranded folk are out at sea, these three actors, and the three must fend for themselves out in open waters.

The crew sit on the couch to watch the film with the pair. A close-up of them all. Seret's face blurred out (too young, or she has not consented for her likeness to be used in perpetuity). *The man sitting on the plastic couch (Burle) is just a plaything really, nothing more*, Mona tells us later. *Yes, we're engaged to be married,* she says, *does this contract require something significant of me?*

Burle is sitting quietly on the couch watching Mona eat the mango. He seems amused and we see this in his demeanor, and in his lips, tilted upward. There's a large age difference between them. They both believe the other to be a plaything, they toy with each other.

Burle asks us later, *isn't Mona fun? Playful?* Mo tells him to his face, *you're just a plaything, you know.* She wants him to feel humiliated. He smiles. Lips blue, purple. The finest teeth in between. The whitest.

The film they are watching shows three faces, two women, and the third face, a man's, is mostly set aside. Sanaa Lathan's face, she treads water, our good friend is in the film. Sanaa Lathan is an actress. She sits on the park bench downstairs, laughing her head off, hair moving violently in the wind. Mona focuses on the mango and the little gap in Sanaa Lathan's teeth onscreen. She ignores the upward movement of Burle's hand, and the downward movement. The three are stranded out in the ocean and the sun is close to setting.

Outside the poplar trees sway almost to the point of snapping. Winds at 70 mph.

Burle is outside of Mona's understanding, he mostly keeps to himself. Though it's easy to understand he's a smooth talker, a womanizer. We've seen his face while planting flowers on the east side. We've observed him curling several women's tendrils around his finger. We know him like we know the pollen, like we know the face of the man in this film—it's Billy Dee Williams—stranded at sea. Stranded with these two women, Sanaa Lathan and another (we don't recognize the other) and these two women will surely drown him.

It is easy to know a nose, a defining characteristic. We know Mona's, her and Von have similar noses, or even the same nose, though one face is old and the other is new. They do resemble each other in a way, though one is old and the other is new, and one is stunning and the other is plain. In the footage one is pregnant, and the other is not.

Their eyes too, the eyelashes are the same, long; *they share the same daddy, you know*, the neighbors say in the laundry room or in the lobby, *different moms but they have the same daddy, that Williams man, Obie, Obie Williams... used to call him Obit, wouldn't he die every season? Collecting his own obituaries like a sport*—though it was never confirmed with a test.

Vonetta!'s momma got around that Nora that's not Mona's momma that one we called her Irene but that Nora was fast loose and for all they know their daddy could've been Billy Dee Williams himself both women have something of Billy Dee don't they? His nose certainly, the neighbors say, though Sanaa Lathan doesn't agree. *For all we know Billy Dee could be their daddy sure enough another Williams man*, but if she hears the gossip Sanaa Lathan defends them, *no no no*.

Mona and Vonetta! both inherited the apartment, their daddy's place. They hold the same surname, and so it also makes sense that they are roommates, life long roommates, or that this shared agreement/space is not really a voluntary thing. The tree is just about gone, the roots almost completely pulled out of the ground—Sanaa Lathan howling on the bench. It's hurricane season. Burle's eyes are closed and his nostrils are open.

When we do it, Mona says looking at the camera head

on, shoulders squared, *right here on the plastic couch that is also my bed, he is wooden, frozen under my weight. I hold Burle's torso with both legs with my knees and his ecstasy is such that he doesn't even move! 'Don't move', I say to him. The plastic making all that noise, riding, and the couch pushing up against the wall.*

The front door slams behind Mona on her way to work. Vonetta! comes out the backroom to find Burle on the couch alone. Beryl has gone to church, Jackie to play the numbers, Seret to hang with the other teens. The camera is propped on the ground, still rolling. There he is, his lower body leaning. *Mo's gone to work*, he says. *Vonny something is stirring can you feel it? Shut the window. And don't you look fine... fine as a fresh batch of clay fine as I ever seen you. So you heard about the thing happened down at the school? You should've seen it. One person deceased not from the fire but from all that water they pushed up into the building. Drowned killed dead. I happened to be down there trying to catch the bus downtown going to East 127th I saw it with my own eyes yes and then Jackson pushed me from behind and I let him have it. We exchanged the fisticuffs. I didn't hurt him just set him straight and then I watched them fuckers pump all that water in pumped too much water in there. Did Seret tell you? Mo? A waterfall coming right out of the school! Matches didn't have nothing to do with it no no... can you fix me something to eat? You know Mona can't cook. The fire department came in late and ready to drown us all.*

The pregnant belly is obscured by the largeness of the shirt, Janet Jackson unsmiling, while Vonetta! marches into the kitchen to make Burle a steak, medium rare and two eggs over easy, grits. He stays watching the film, Billy Dee Williams is gone, submerged, already perished. From the television set we hear Sanaa Lathan acting her heart out, *I don't have to do nothing but stay black and die!*, and we know the film is almost coming to an end.

THE DIVINITY OF NEON ORANGE.

The art is in the windows... oh hell, the windows are covered or taped up with construction paper, or with instructions for assembling furniture. Look at this, our windows covered with family photographs. A photo of Net's mother eating cake with Net's daddy, and with Mo's daddy, Sanaa Lathan says, laying the cards out for solitaire.

See how the neighborhood art extends from window to window, across buildings, to the vacant lots that surround us. There are murals and temporary installations sitting in lots, the light installations, all kinds of stuff. And the artists are plentiful, old artists, and also men, young men, and young people. Around the vacant lots there is space enough to reveal a monument, or something awe-inspiring, though nothing is currently being exhibited due to the Holiday.

Charlie's window is covered—showcasing photographs of uncles in bathing suits for example, or a cousin, Trina bending her knees, or some page from a magazine (Sade Adu on the cover of i-D Magazine, Issue 14, 1983; one eye closed) zines, prints, encyclopedic offerings, neon orange construction paper, materials found in the libraries.

Sanaa Lathan has come over to chat, or to spend the night. *It is said that public spaces have changed—a library is not what it once was!*, Sanaa Lathan hollers.

She leans from the window to yell out to passersby: *I like that hat girl, I like those shoes, where did you get them shoes?* The mic does not pick up a response. Sanaa turns to say, *a community center a supermarket or a stadium is not what it once was, no no no. But the libraries are still useful, the neighbors fornicate in them, but isn't it wonderful, too, that anyone can walk into a library, take one page from the remaining books, bring it home with them to decorate a window?*

Where's Beryl?
At the market?
Call Beryl.

Children yelling from art-filled windows—*the library is not what it once was!*

There are statues here and there—Vonetta! picks up the monologue—*mostly figures of women carved into stone. They hold things: a book, a gavel, a torch, or a food item. They cannot be hands-free, see, the feminine figures must juggle something or they must be shown multi-tasking...*

Vonetta! and Mona sit on the living room carpet with pillows under their arms and behind the knees, and with the cardboard boxes scattered. A deck of cards. There is so much to unpack—the items being unearthed. Sanaa Lathan sitting atop the piano stool. Mona rubbing Vonetta!'s scalp. They watch a film, it's always the same. *Is the child kicking?* Vonetta!'s stomach moves like an ocean, like so. Sanaa Lathan's child, Lira, sleeps on the bed in the backroom.

They watch the three people stranded at sea. Treading water. When the film is in its third act a climax is reached. The two stranded women look over at the stranded man and decide something. They're all very dehydrated, there isn't any time to fuck around. They don't have to say aloud what choice they've come to. They sing a hymn, or something. A call and response. *The man must go*, the hymn seems to say, or *we must use him for our own survival*.

Things end badly for the man, Billy Dee. The women cheer, *amen amen*, though the circumstances remain dire. Mona rubbing Vonetta!'s scalp, Sanaa Lathan rubbing Mo's scalp, and Vonetta! rubbing down Sanaa's feet as the credits roll.

The jobs that remain available on the Hill involve repair, Vonetta! says unprompted, *plumbers are of use and if you want to keep objects as they are there is plenty of work to be had. Keep the existing pipes, to sustain what's already in place and keep it functioning is okay. To maintain the status quo is fine. To be a journalist is alright, but to be a revolutionary is not. The downstairs neighbor is a journalist.*

Inventing is akin to sinning!, the journalist neighbor, Bobby (real name Bubba) likes to say while washing his clothes in the laundry room.

Invention is akin to sinning!, the high-schoolers say on their way to the school building. The school building has been burnt down to its foundation.

A politician is okay, Vonetta! continues. *An actress can use her role to reflect the norms of society or some of the violence. A seamstress can mend, sure. It's okay to mend or fix things, to hammer them together; that is allowed. In other words, to take care of (in minor ways) the objects or people that need tending to is encouraged. But creating something altogether new—no. No. To be innovative is to be out of line, darling. 'Things are meant to break' the government says, 'there is divinity in what is broken and in the broken is the divine!'*

The orange sky, the orange sky is reflected in the lake and in the cars moving past. From up top, from this height here there is the impression of stillness. From the second highest floor of the tallest apartment building there is absence.

Sanaa Lathan lives on the floor above, the seventeenth, the highest, the last, but she is over at Vonetta!'s house enough that it seems as if she rooms there too. *She brings her little boy down to take his naps in the backroom, or to eat, or to quiet down.*

It is said that the gods have bestowed the architecture upon us, or that the neon orange paint is divine. Buildings are made up in this neon orange, Sanaa Lathan exclaims.

And the salt marshes below, dammit, they're sinking.

Dammit, we repeat.

There is an eighth of an inch of sinking every three to six months. *There's nothing to be done about it*, Mona says, playing with the diamond ring on her ring finger, *this place is inhospitable, there will be migration or movement. And some are already preparing to leave... we left for a short while.*

When the women left for the short while, just for the week, they packed up their shit quick, erected the cardboard boxes, stuffed things in storage; they left us. They left for a week but had to return when the money ran out. And when they came back, bleeding, tired, unpacking/unpacking/unpacking, we welcomed them.

The government won't assist any of the folk who choose to leave or opt out. There is no funding for relocation. The government goes out of their way to reassure us that the area is safe and that the zone isn't in any real jeopardy. It is sinking, yes, true enough, but it is also painted in a neon orange, and when the sun sets it is a similar kind of orange, and is that not the work of a higher power?

CHATTER.

You?
 No, not me.
 Who?
 Vonetta! and Burle when they used to be a thing moons ago many moons ago. She claims they were married once and aren't they expecting a child? Where is the child?
 Now it's Burle and Mona goddamn.
 Everyone knows it.
 Yeah! Yeah.
 Do they sound out again?
 Yeah. Oh, yeah.
 I hear the... banging—
 I can't sleep. I can't catch a wink of sleep. They've been at it for hours mercy. And I have heard it said that Burle... Burle as a pottery artist or ceramic artist or whatever he was got him knowing something about water. That he knows water well or that he knows the mud mud is obvious to him and he has a familiarity with dampness with humidity, with how to apply pressure... its gradual shift. Mind you they bring their hands up up in reverse when they create an ashtray or whatever it spins around and around and they use these tools to make ridges on a vase or to smooth it over into a phallic shape. The kiln. I have heard it said—he seems to know about movement a pedal a spinning—
 Opening a thing up.
 Mhmm. Fingers all dirty. Water... water takes/took my baby. The firefighters wouldn't stop with the double-layered hose. They pumped it in with the high test pressure and the high durability even when the fire was over and done with.
 It's a shame, such a shame—
 A real goddamn shame! I had to clean the mud from up under her fingernails before the repast. Took me days—

Burle that's what he was/is a ceramic artist?
Yes. Well he isn't that now.
Maybe not anymore. But he was?
Yes, he was.
Oh.

Walking around with mud under his fingernails. And back in the day he had Vonetta! eating dirt right on up from the earth in the garden. Fistfuls of dirt! He had her losing her mind, lost her the job.

I bet he still drives her up the wall going over to see Mona at all hours and telling Vonetta! to fix him some eggs and ham hocks and shit.

She was eating the earth! Planting her trees, seeds in her pockets, walking around barefoot or on all fours, and snacking on the earth!

And she's still carrying his things. Do you think she'll go into labor?

I don't know. We don't know.

It's fitting. She is belabored, a piece of work.

Yes... though it is a blessing.

A mother is usually the one wearing the child on the waist, is she not? We've never seen a father carry a thing.

What do fathers carry? Pocket change?

The trunk of the paper birch tree as soft as a child's belly, and the forty yard line, the first down, sour...

He's unhoused I hear.

I don't know, he could be. He has his tent but always seems to find a bed to lay in at night. Yes. He's set up a good dry space for himself out there near the city hall. A blue tent. He knows how to erect a thing, Burle. And I suppose that there is something to his punctuality.

There is that. It's a gift to be so punctual...

Wide-shouldered.

He's always showing up on time to the meetings, to the

festivities, and all through the major Holiday.

If you tell him 'come at 6 p.m.' that man will show up at 17:35. Hell... the lilies opened up today.

Yeah?

Yeah. They'll be dead by tomorrow afternoon, the government says.

You know better than to pass on their thin rhetoric. I'll go see the lilies in the morning.

Yeah you should you should go see them in the morning.

I will.

And burn some incense in here or something, the air is heavy.

Alright.

It's heavy in here. Means things are coming, I think.

What's coming?

I don't know, things.

Mmm...

Burle looks good for his age don't he?

He does. He does.

Like I said it's in the shoulders.

Mhmm.

The width of them—

Here they go again.

With an open hand too.

Mmhmm.

And what's she yelling out? What's that Mo keeps calling out? Tries to be all proper with her government job but still calling out like a green heifer. Can you tell? Get closer to the wall.

It sounds like she's saying... balloon.

Balloon?

Balloon.

And it sound to me like she's lying flat on her back. Plastic sticking and unsticking.

They'll be done soon enough, he is nothing if not punctual! It's a shame whew. What a damn shame...

It's windy.
Weather is turning.
Sure is, sure is...

The national game being broadcast to all televisions simultaneously, familiar men, no children—

And can you see Vonetta! from the window and the belly and the child and Sanaa's child? She's babysitting Lira.

I think so yes. Someone is planting something right down in the front. Lira is probably asleep next to her, in her lap, or on the bench.

Sanaa's child's is lying down right on the dirty bench.
But can you see the belly from the window? Any part of it?
No.
That baby boy is never coming, lord have mercy.

We don't know that we don't know anything. We're not no doctors! It's God's will and the child will come out when he's good and ready. The water will break... that child knows something about water, he's been submerged for ages he knows water well or he for sure he knows the mud mud is obvious to him he is damp he has some familiarity with dampness or with humidity or with the pressure. Maybe the good Lord does not find Von! to be ready. He'll come out when he's good and ready or when He commands it. And children are separate from us. No one understands it, they are separate... And sometimes they're just tall for their age stretched out or otherwise too small for their age or they want to stay where they're at.

Unnatural is what I call it...

I don't want to hear nothing more about it, the child is just shy. The last one said it's healthy, it's just stretched out or too small to come out. And to be stretched out is to be closer to Him, and to be small is to be closer to the earth—

Now the child is divine?

Yes, maybe so. To have such limbs, small or stretched, is to bring one closer to the neon orange.
Lord have mercy... what's for dinner?
I took the lamb out of the freezer.
Lamb?
The rack of lamb for the Holiday. With the potatoes—
Did you hear that Milly?
He's gone. Burle's come and gone.

TEMPORARY FIXINGS.

There is the major Holiday—a celebration of something past, of which these folks are only vaguely familiar. We do not fully understand its origin, but we know what is tradition. Ribbons are involved, purple. Things are painted, candied, covered. Someone is assigned to record the footage, edit it, splice it with the old footage, make copies, distribute it to the mailboxes. Often enough, the fog will come in and the clouds will come down; that is part of it.

If the sky is very very orange it is a sign to retire to our beds. Otherwise, it will be a week of exaltation, or of sitting and watching the film.

The buildings of the Hill can seem mountainous. And if you happen to get a glimpse of the space between the buildings while climbing the asphalt—there's a minute of greenery or of ice in between. Daffodils. The urban landscape is met with small mounds, and we've mentioned the hills before. It takes people hours to travel through the valley to reach it, especially if coming into town on foot. It takes even longer to arrive by bus, though if you own a car it can be scenic/serene. The highways cut right through mountains, beige mountains or snow capped mountains. The clouds hanging so low. There is traffic, so much traffic, but the drive is worthwhile and comes highly recommended.

All the boxes (the air conditioner boxes), sticking out of the apartment windows like moles from a face, or skin tags from a neck, acrochordons—seen from quite a distance.

There they go, thousands of boxes sticking out pointless to remove and reinstall so we mostly leave them in. Steeples sticking up from those places of worship and posters advertising a semi-naked body. A church, quiet and charred. All this can be found from the second highest window, or as you approach the Hill on that very scenic drive, but only vaguely for the fog is always there on the major Holiday, and the clouds hang low.

The citizens/community are dressed to the nines.

Stockings and bulbous knits. Knee-high boots, those that reach the calf, or even the thigh if one can pull it off. Two-piece bikinis are appropriate, wings made from goose feathers are encouraged. The wardrobe depends on the season, which is often unpredictable and sporadic.

On this occasion of the major Holiday it is hot, warm, and the meals have already been prepared; there is music. *In the air: aromatics, fish soup, lentils.* Journey Through "The Secret Life of Plants" *playing on repeat. We're anxious to participate in good faith.*

Every year, once a year the bells sound. *Light the incense with a pocket lighter press the oils into the skin*, Sanaa Lathan says.

At 23:30, Tuesday, things move, things are written down, understand?

Vonetta! writing something on scraps of paper, in black ink, and the air conditioner boxes are taken out of windows (only this once) for the scraps to be thrown from their openings.

If you prefer a flower can be thrown.

It doesn't need to be explained, it's done anonymously. What is expected of the Holiday is something precipitous or capricious. No one recycles. Snow-like, thin materials. We capture the scraps falling/falling/falling down from above and it is the same as always.

At 00:00, Wednesday, the move to street level begins, to pick up a scrap or to pocket a thing that fell most likely from a neighbor. To pick up a lily stem, Vonetta! says.

The Holiday is about communal codependency and that's what outsiders can't grasp. Outside we are hot and hauling ass, racing barefoot, with uncles who used to run track fucking up their knees: an ACL torn to shreds.

We take turns piling into the elevators or into the stairwells, we run from the street with grease shining on our skin, on our foreheads, climbing the flight of stairs with boots covering the varicose veins, bending just a minute before to gather a scrap of fallen paper or a flower, or to whistle in the cold, in the hot, to smoke. We pile back into the elevator or into stairwells. It takes long, back and forth, or however long it must.

We gather to watch the old footage, spliced together with some new footage. It runs for hundreds of hours. *The infrastructure sinks around us, everything in disrepair.*

Jackson the plumber likes to lollygag on the major Holiday. Likes to sit down whole, a week of sitting, he won't land on his feet at all, not once, and he drinks soda water, lime, and whiskey, eating with both hands, real slow like, listening to the gossip.

Sanaa Lathan likes to braid everyone's hair on the major Holiday, so we take turns sitting between her. We feel her breath on our scalp and on the back of our neck. Sanaa Lathan brings up some scandal or another, *the fire at the school,* she says, *the fire at the church, the fire at the warehouse. The drowned girl in her uniform skirt, all bloated. There were two deaths from all the water they pumped in. Milly's child, yes*, she says into their waiting heads, *the other one has not yet been identified.*

People air out their grievances, or they tease each other. *You look like a bug-eyed so and so*, they say. Or they call each other heifers. *You're a dirty sloppy dusty dumb as a rock low-down dirty man-eating heifer.* It's sophisticated the way they curse each other out. *Goddamn you motherfucker.*

Bragging, calling each other's bluffs, shouting from the window, lollygagging, and embellishing like hell.

The mosquitos feasting. The men playing dominoes.

Burle is dressed to the nines, draped down, classy like. He yells out, *I shot him lightly, and he died politely!*

Mona, smoking a marijuana cigarette.

Milly smoking a marijuana cigarette.

Vonetta! swiveling her hips around, gyrating, teasing, cutting a rug, and the child in her belly no longer weighing her down. Some hands resting on her for good luck, others giving up the gesture. All that is left then is to eat, to devour. It is customary to sit down low to the floor on a pillow or on the carpet, or to lean against the plastic of a couch, and they do. *We do*, and later we move to the rooftop, sleeping bags afoot. One on top of the other, or head to foot. We eat and sleep in fits and then there is a point of no return or of quieting down, not talking, only eating or sleeping, or humming or listening. It goes far into the night and into the next day, still the Wednesday.

We listen to Slum Village. Diana Ross is dressed up for Richard Pryor's funeral, we fix the lighting and the backlighting.

In the beginning the major Holiday was about a man, Hill, whoever he was or aimed to be, not as it is now about this film, or his descendants, the neighbors, Mona, Vonetta!, Earla Mae, Jackie, Ernestine, Z, Morris, Seret, Everton, Cherylin, Milly, Beryl, Sanaa Lathan, Linda Sharrock, and the others.

And what, we wonder still, has the community become? Why have we continued with this? What do we want to hear? What are the decibels of our surroundings? Do we feel the sinking? Kids too tired to sleep, anxious to play tag. Is the lady from the first floor who never moved to higher ground under the mud ? It is after 02:00 and what of the wind?

If anything is to be said during the meal (that is not sung) it is read aloud from a scrap of paper thrown from a window and collected outside—one chosen at 03:07 reads: *everything in disrepair, everything is taped together, temporary fixings. Small genocides. Existential Freedom + Responsibility.*

These offerings are not intended to be profound. Those who participate in this thing are lucky, it seems.

Are we lucky? we ask the room.

The Holiday is meant to offer a quiet reminder, we are born with a spoon in our mouths, even in this crumbling place, a lady says, maybe Jackie, as she climbs to the roof.

The way the sun sets: it is what it has always been, long/ temporary. The sun comes and goes in ways both ridiculous and uncalled for. The poplar trees move, their seeds move. We have finally decided to cut them down at the bust. And the highways were moved to cover the busts of women no longer celebrated, statues with a neck exposed covering us with little shade. The bridge has been lowered a few more centimeters to stop the public buses from reaching the beach. The poppy seeds are lost at sea but we are comfortable, blessed, to watch the children pulling at the okra.

OLD ASS ARCHITECTURE.

[A close up on Vonetta!'s leg.] A thick leg, muscular. Outside, lines or a place of recognition. The leg is seen because Vonetta! is tying her shoes. Her laces are always coming undone. *Isn't the leg a line?* Tying the laces. And the woman's name: Vonetta! *Vonetta!.* Or fast. *Fast-thing,* Fast is the name the neighbors use when her leg sticks out of place. Sometimes they call her by her last name, *Williams.* Or worse, *a damned whore. That thick ass leg is out of place for a woman! An old woman at that. The musculature is out of place for how the body should be presented oh! We admire it. Especially this body of a woman in their golden years, though it is difficult to tell her age 65? 75? 88? We regard her body. Hasn't she been around for all of time? Hasn't she been around? 105? A woman of 90 hair bone white.*

And some of the skin on Williams' leg being shown out of context (outside the pleasure of a man) that's when the neighbors take it upon themselves to call out a name that isn't really hers or to talk about the fullness of her ass, the pregnant belly, the protrusion of the top lip, full, the bottom, the hips—*the whole sordid sexuality of her old ass body.*

LATENESS.

Vonetta! or fast-thing or Williams (henceforth: the mother) is late. Things are always ahead of her.

The curtain blows and she knows it's winter. The living room is painted white. There are outlets in each of the walls. The camera shifts away from her and toward the view of the lake, the salt marsh. An artificial lake, a swamp, or something. The high school (*burnt down*) is beside the cemetery and right beside the burnt church. The library. The burnt warehouse. The teens hollering on their way to grab lunch.

The body, the body of water lapping; the boats giving out splinters.

It's a cloudy day; *it seems always to be cloudy lately*, the mother says. Earlier, when she had walked to the grocery store the seagulls had raced her. The geese chased her, the men walking three steps behind.

The mother cleans the kitchen counter while the child Sanaa Lathan bore on the floor of the hospital room sleeps. The mother is a godmother to this child, named Lira. Sanaa Lathan believes Lira is just old enough to take care of itself. (*S. L. and Lira are captured from a low angle, not straight on, a Dutch angle, a two-shot.*)

Sanaa Lathan is tired, *sometimes*, of caring for someone outside of herself. The mother is tired too, dehydrated and hung-over; late—and when we talk about lateness, it isn't about showing up behind the others. Her lateness is one of sincerity—she sees things as they are. She is only late because everyone else wants to have the upper hand! They all want to live in the near future.

The mother does not aim for this, she does not think about being avant-garde. The church bells ring every fifteen minutes.

It is 12:00, precisely 12. *It's the middle of the day, Thursday, the weather at its peak, and it is warm, seasonably so, not unseasonably so, it should be said that the warmth is right, fair, it is hot as hell, seasonably so, as this has been the weather for the past decade, this very warm weather is the norm and the bitter chill from ten and a half minutes ago is the norm too.*

The cold that hits down to the bone is the norm, depending. The sunlight hits the mother's hand. The mother, she's in the elevator, she goes down to get the mail, bills, junk, then she's back up, pushing the button, she is unlocking the front door, she steps inside of her place. It smells of white sage.

She moves to the window. From her place she looks down (*there is something to be said about looking down from a high place*), and she is feverish.

From the window, the mother finds the man below, Burle. To see a practical stranger so far down, what of it? It's nice. Or it's fine, it's safe. And that's what he is to her, just a stranger, or an acquaintance, someone she sees a couple of times a week. Someone the neighbors believe she is set to have a child with, nothing more. She's known him since she was a child—there's no space between them. They are peers.

Her up high and the stranger/acquaintance down below.

And what is it about the middle of the day? *It's a privilege to do things of your own choosing in the very middle of the day. To be home alone. Everyone is out.* The air is clean-ish in the apartment high up, the new air purifier is running on a low setting. The mother's thighs are spread apart, to inspect but also to feel something akin to confidence. There is confidence in moving one's legs in a provocative way. To move a mature pair of gams in the very middle of the day while sitting on a plastic couch, thighs spread, fingers spreading—*it's good*.

The job is lost. There is nothing to it, the offer was rescinded, or the position was eliminated. She was eliminated sixty months ago. *Inventing is akin to sinning!*, the higher-ups said. *To be innovative is to be out of line, ma'am*, they said. *Things are meant to break, there is divinity in what is broken.*

There is money from the government, weekly checks. In a few days the money will come again in the mail. In the middle of the day she lounges.

Cum for me.

This is what she was taught, by the porn industry, by the men, to the men, and this is how she speaks. She does not use this language with the women. The neighbors think her to be vulgar, the neighbors call her fast, a *fast thing, fast, fresh*.

The mother was raised with words that are open or straightforward. Her mom raised her to be open or straightforward, and her daddy, Obit, her cousin Nichelle, her uncle Tulle, all her aunties. *There isn't any shame in it, not in language*, so she does not feel it. She does it. *On the couch, if you like.*

The old couch used to be filthy, but this new one is pristine. *Seven years with the plastic on it and still practically new*, the mother says. *It's pristine and noisy, see? and underneath the plastic it's as white as can be. Bone white.*

She's forward, the neighbors say into the lavalier mic.

The apartment is pristine but functional. There are one and a half bedrooms, a kitchen all white—white appliances—a baby grand piano (*there is function in a baby grand*), and there are containers on the kitchen counter that hold a few grams of sugar (white and brown, respectively), coarse salt, Manuka honey, chickpea flour, turmeric. The living room belongs to Mona.

In the middle of a Thursday, during the proceedings for the Holiday everyone is gathering. Mona gathering the community center drawings, Seret near the lake with the teens gathering leaves, plants. The building is quiet.

She closes the thighs. The child does not kick. She closes everything up. She undresses and dresses again.

It's empty out when she begins to wash the hallway floors. The mother moves up and down, side to side. The film crew (3) moves around her. *There's a technique to this*, the mother says. For the mother, it is the most preferable of chores, washing the floors, *it's satisfying because of the movement, all the back and forth*, she says, *but it's also the fact of washing/clearing a shared space, the hallways are for everybody, sometimes I even wash down the stairs, hundreds of flights of stairs, or the elevator floor, which is filthy as can be, all the way down to the sidewalk or to the courtyard, with soapy water and a broom, and the sound—the whoosh, and the bristles and the roughness of material upon material.*

The water splashing, spilling into the neck of my socks.

And what is it about bending down to tie your shoe? It feels productive, innate, it is a nostalgic thing to bend down and tie one's laces in the same way as you have ever done it, the mother says, *always the same, elbows out, looping twice.*

On her body the most comfortable of materials, breathable materials.

The books of the apartment are plentiful. On the coffee table, a cover filled with plants, along with the exterior of a brutalist building, *Urban Planning!*, the title says, *Landscape Architecture!* Within the book, page seven, the photo of a hallway.

The mother stole the book from the job from which she was eliminated six months ago. And they gave her the runaround. There seemed to be something about her that they hadn't cared for, or something they had grown tired of (her blackness). *We expect more from someone of your stature.*

The higher ups wouldn't give her adequate time for lunch, for example, or any time to sit away from her desk and consume things: candy bars, candied yams, dirt. *You are here to work*, they would say, *not to fuck around.*

But everything came easy and the tasks were finished in record time. Her work was lauded. They didn't like that, it seemed, or the candy wrappers that piled up and gathered in her lap, or in her desk drawers; the grass stains on her knees.

Or the way she took long to research the projects, the irrigation and drainage systems. Or her overall lateness, nor the way she spread her things/thighs everywhere when she sat—at her desk or at a conference table—*which is the way I'd always been taught to sit: comfortably, to spread my things/thighs, or to make myself known.*

And the bathroom breaks, which were plentiful. The pressure on her bladder constant and easy. They all dreaded the prospect of what her maternity leave might look like, endless, like the pregnancy, *endless*, they said.

The mother drinks a ton of water, she was born in water, in a small inflatable pool set up in the living room of the apartment where she now lives. The mother's mother, Mrs. Williams, had insisted upon it while giving birth, and performing this most natural thing in water, with the bottom half of her in water, squatting, and those present said that one baby swam around with the umbilical cord still tethering them, *and the other baby*, they said, *was born real quiet/unswimming.*

The mother drinks club soda, sparkling, mineral, natural, still, flavored; tea with lime or lemon, grapefruit or orange slices, with bitters. Not whiskey like Jackson likes, or whiskey with milk like Jackie likes, just plain old water. She gulps it down. Which reminds us that there's no water in the house, none at all, and she refuses to drink the tap water, though everyone else drinks it.

I'll buy a house somewhere, with a pool in its backyard, fitted into the earth, in-ground. And when one is immersed in a pool and leaning their arms on the edge, she says, *with chin on hands and elbows set wide, with feet kicking behind; that's what I want, sometimes or most of all.*

The hallway smells of citrus. She carries the bucket and dumps the brown liquid down the drain. The dirt goes down, *down*.

She waits in the hall for the elevators to hum, for doors to slam, for the click-clacking of shoes, for the smell of cooking, or the banging of garbage as it moves through the chute, for Mona, *Mo, Simona*; or for Sanaa/Lathan.

16:05, the jangling of keys. The yelling, the neighbors don't have patience, they yell, their feet are throbbing. The high-schoolers returning.

The mother moves her locs into a ponytail. *To wash any floor or to perform any chore, to plant some seeds, to gather some grass, the hair must be set away from the rest of the body*, the mother says, *off of the shoulders, or pinned back from the forehead*.

When she gathers the coils, with the heaviness of the hair and the large green scrunchie on her wrist, her arms are already tired from the effort. Green scrunchie on the right wrist pulled forward, over the right hand, the left hand pulling it through, looping it around, around the flesh of the left hand, then looping back around the fingers, the right index finger holding taut, releasing.

There is relief in things done well, done thoroughly or with care, the mother says... *It is a sin to consume a well-done steak! This section of hallway is pristine,* she quiets down to say.

Most have returned, the neighbors filling up the assigned spaces. 17A, 18J, 10B, 4C. *On the thigh, the inner part of the thigh*—what she hears is the moan—a plate, or something ceramic breaking upon wood. She slides a chair out into the hallway, she wants to hear them come. The walls are plain, the floors are checkered.

Everything is sinking. What is to become of the labyrinth?

The layouts of all the apartments are identical, sometimes reversed but always the same. The measurements are the same.

And these 55,000 residents, what of them? Who will care for all the hallways that adjoin them? Who will care for the most vulnerable? The old, the disabled, the children? The janitors have been recruited for science. The janitors are busy, gone. And what of the other wings and hallways and courtyards and common spaces?

Her hair wrapped into a bun, she takes joy in braiding the cheese. In the folded chair she braids it. She begins in the long kitchen of course: the cheese curds, the hot water. Then, she braids them. When she's done she packs everything up; she delivers them to the neighbors.

The paper boxes tied and wrapped up into cloth materials, with a pebble or a rock (soaked in vinegar) placed on the inside, a token; and for dinner she has decided on prawns. Prawns with the heads left on. A slice of lime. When the twelve neighbors on the sixteenth floor open up the boxes they are delighted: pepper prawns, mozzarella, lime wedges, olive oil, coarse salt, honey, a rock collected from the lake that feeds into the salt marsh.

Have you ever placed a beach towel on a rock near a body of water and laid down upon it? The rocks were formed before us... to lie on a rock is to understand something more about discomfort, or accepting what is. Downstairs the grass, the moss, *the grasses are dry and yellow... Weeds, weeds.*

Yellow, or golden, like wood can be golden. And furniture made of wood is cut, molded, sewed, finished. There is so much the mother wants to understand: the process of cutting up some wooden furniture, its molding, sewing, setting. She wants to know things the way she knows the landscape.

The pine trees swaying. And the name is Vonetta!, she says *Vonetta!, Vonetta!*, when she faces the camera, *don't call me the mother*, she doesn't want a nickname, a shorthand, *It's Vonetta!*, she says when she introduces herself to any man or woman, or child.

PART II, *the text*

RIGHT THIGH:

the letters of an alphabet pressed from petals, stretch mark of an a b c, blind hem stitching, or the old scars forced to call.
a mother and a   child, 1999, a present little child and a soon to be mother. Are   mothers
the center? The neighbor Sanaa, she is a mother, a mom. That babe   of hers,   Lira,
he believes that they are each other's center, and he understands, too,   that neither of
them have a   choice. We know the mother and the child, the child?   yes, and
the   neighbors, a whale, a
wailing   godmother,
it's   settled. This connection that a mother
sometimes   has with their
born/   unborn   children or
*   that the   average babe (born/unborn)*
*   has with a   mother,   is*
it   taken for granted? Or doesn't
everyone   know
*   about it? Not everything is innate, or*
*   understood, but for a*
mother to   be the
center, for the   offspring to be the center
*   does not   necessarily mean that*
the   relationship is healthy in
any way,   shape, or   form!
The pair is simply involved in a   way that is
*   final. This is it   for me. There's*
nothing more to it. There's   nothing more
between   us. Most   are
not interested   in children, in having them

or   acknowledging them, or treating
          them in a   normal   way,
so they cannot understand—   you cannot.
          Sorry to say, but you have chosen a   life, to remain
as   you are, and it should be
          mentioned that there is some resentment there—
sorry to say, but I never would have   done
it,   never.   and there is regret, oh, my Gunn, who is
often left to his own devices;
he's a lonely child. My poor child, he plays his lonely games,
he is so bored, so goddamn bored,   pushing
the   plastic bubble down with all his weight,
trouble, and he doesn't even   know me, he's too young
to know   me,   except for the innate
knowledge that   the mother figure is not the kind
of   mother he would choose. Yes. And
as for me, as for   me? I simply wish to go back to a
life of not   solving a thing—a life of findable
hours.
Burle, Burle, Bur, birth name Jackson Burle Erudite
Jackson—Jackson Jackson, JJ, a man   who
used to be a ceramicist, a potter, and still is, we see the hairs
around   the mouth, we   are so close to
him, zooming in, a single   shot, and his skin is sublime, even
as his hands are cursed   with   arthritis and
with psoriasis, so dry from the constant
washing of them. What he used to
create in his prime were objects too heavy to hold up—six
feet high,
   huge bowls,   huge,   too
big   vessels, vases, frames; among many
other things, many many other   things.   Some
of   them   still
exist in a cupboard or a museum. But   he is

*unencumbered now,
unmoored and he   sometimes lives outdoors when
not in   the company of a partner or a
friend. He camps out. He   does not think of
the objects, except   when he is reminded of
them by a   sibling, by a
neighbor, or distant cousin.
    The smell of resin   will remind him, or
when he sees the   piece at   Mo's
house, the one he gave to me, to me, and on occasion
I'm   reminded   while
drying my   hands with a paper towel, or a
terry cloth towel—that   will bring me
    right back to   it. Burle remembers the
size, shape, depth,   overall   weight
and circumference of each piece he   has ever made.
    Burle is alive, he has friends who visit him almost every
day, every other day. Or he visits   them,
        the women and men, he seduces them all. He plays
games, spades, dominos, gin   rummy,
dice,   poker, blackjack. He shifts the cards around
real good and easy. When Burle is   in the
company of   Lathan and the child, or the mother, the
woman, a new possibility opens up for   him,
or   a new avenue of life is
revealed: a family. But he cannot stand it for long,
which is why Burle   slams the door on his
way   out or it's why he makes a beeline
for Mona on the couch, mango   in hand. We
are not even done   with him, and   there
he goes slamming the door, bam. Or   he tells Mo to
meet him in   the tent   downstairs, or
at the glass paned community center. When   he
is back in his royal blue tent   what he feels*

most acutely is relief/release.
And speaking of Mona, Mo, who we see but know very little about, she has a reputation for　　　　　　　　being good in bed. Those interviewed for the film, long ago, as part of our　　　field　　　work, field notes, they　　　mentioned only this one thing, 'Mona is good in bed', they said,　　　so we chastised them and spoke　　to them of misogyny.
And　　　when we　　　spoke to Mona she said it, right into the mic, I'm good. We don't know much else　　　　　　about her, we only know of her taste for mangoes, her compulsions to eat any that are left in　　　the large wooden bowl, and we know of the way she forces Burle　　　　to remain
　very still. We know she is young enough, younger than Burle and many years　　　younger than　　　　me. We do not know much about her work, though some say Mona makes　　　six figures, seven, working for the state. Others believe she works two jobs or three, we　　　　don't know.　　Her skin is　　　dark and soft with fine hairs, though she has　　　excised them completely　　　from　　　her body with a laser. She weighs ___ lbs, we know only that she's　　　perfect. Medium　　　breasts, small hands,　　　　liv-ing on and around a plastic couch,　　　long legs; the breadwinner, paying　　all the　　　　bills in the house.

　(Don't you know Leanne, Bootsy, Earla Mae, Ernestine, Duane, Morris, Hakeem, Z, Milly, Marpessa, Joyce, Nichelle,　　　Bobby　　　and them who are mentioned more as a collective and seen more　　as a collection, but　　　are interesting individuals, no doubt about it, in and of themselves.　　　They each

*pursue their own separate interests, jobs, hobbies, during the
major Holiday they each have their   own small
    pleasures, Marpessa eating banana pudding real
slow like, etc., and they each   offer
different   realities and perspectives. They use the
words: copacetic, tight, phat,   diggity, old
words. They each mean well.)*

   *It is important to note the makeup of this place. We have
reached a point   of no return, and
it must be   mentioned: The community is made up of
predominantly black people, 97%   or
93%,   it's a place we've created for ourselves,
okay? Or a place we were forced into   and have
    reimagined.
And I don't know what to make of this makeshift   family. I don't know at all what to make of the
sounds that   come from the apartment,
 these   guttural sounds—it's just
       some arguing—but I
     don't get all the fussing and   carrying on!
'Why can't we   all just share the man in peace?' they shout
out, or holler,   Jesus Christ
    almighty. And when the sounds begin in the mid-
     afternoon they either listen in through
the walls   or sneak   past the hounds, into the
    apartment with the spare   key, mostly to
    check on me, old ass Vonetta!   and her
growing body. Or they sit   on the white
    plastic couch; they admire
the home, which is clean and well cared for. When they are
over,   rubbing   my
belly down down with vaseline or witch hazel, it
    doesn't kick.   They let me sleep or they
wake me up, depending, and they sometimes   feed*

*   me   the dinner that's been prepared*
and left out, fried mackerel or something,   soft
things,   fried   plantain, and the
sounds continue around us.
   There's someone that has barely been   mentioned.
Seret. Seret,   and we can't leave her out.
Seret   Scott, who time ago decided to stay as she
was/is, and she remains so. She was   a
     teenager then and   she is a teenager now.
She decided this, some forty odd   years ago, fifty,
   that her life would be made in the eleventh grade,
and that is the way that   her life has remained [illegible].
     She is an academic, you see, and she   remains so.
  Seret and Sanaa and Beryl and Jackie and myself, we know
each other from back in the day, we   didn't
go to   the high   school together, Beryl
and Jackie were younger, and Sanaa was   the
youngest of us, the five of us, they called us The
     Five   Horsemen, Mo was not yet born.
thirty years   ago, forty-   five,
we've known   each
other in   the   intimate ways that
young people can know one another,
breathing all up in each other's   faces;
but   that's done.   Jackie is dead,
Sanaa's mouth is glued to the bottle, Beryl, dead.
Seret remains as is. We   would sit so close to
   the other, our   five faces touching,
                        breathing down each

other's necks,
 sweaty   and sticking, sticky. And this
   closeness   persisted, persists in a
different form—And even if it didn't look right,   for
me   to get old,   hanging

around an eleventh grader, and for an eleventh grader (who should have turned to adult-hood but has decided to stay as she is/was) to hang with us, these older women, we remained as thick as thieves. People talked. Seret, director of the film. Seret, wearing her hair in a French roll in the back, scrunch set in the front.
   There's landscape. We see it. It has been described in detail and showcased in many of the scenes. It used to be something with order but now it's unruly. It's undone in a way, or redone, free? There is still tradition in it, and in other things [redacted] there is
   the major Holiday to contend with, of course, and that is something that is celebrated by all without exception. But there's a sense of chaos, too, of chaotic individualism, an every man for himself kind of attitude, or an underlying agreement that all men will be selfish if push comes to shove; and the way the asphalt is laid out in this haphazard way and the ways the government doesn't give a flying fuck about us at all, all, all is somewhat tragic. The government especially doesn't care about the 93% who live near a lake and a swamp. There is chaos and sinking, okay? But the residents have made something. We care for it when we use neon orange paint or when we see how the asphalt is like a

    little hill to be   climbed, and when we
feel everything sinking   around
us. This place where the trash is dumped, they
organize us, organize   the hell out of the city
dump. They   plant things. We plant things.
We're included,   We're complicit. The buildings
with   an air   conditioner in every
window and the colorful   paper/photos governing
them. We like   the smell in the air: smoke, lilies,
il babà.   We like the unhoused (who set up
their sea   of tents everywhere and help to
keep the place   safe).
 It should be reiterated: it's not only me, Vonetta! Amethyst
Williams, who pays attention to the mud.   This
obsession with nature—all   all all of the Hill carries
it! Our   landscape—it
is low and high! It's a deep   thing, and there are
valleys, yes, the   smog,
fog, lakes, swamps, the unrecyclable, geese that don't migrate/
get the hell on, we filmed the   geese,
slow,   their angel wings formed from eating too
much goddamn bread. The   leaves: respected/
preserved by the community, all the way down to the root,
whatever still   exists and
you know, the mussels, silkworms on the clover and dandelion,
  and despite the atmospheric dissonance
the   poppy seeds are spread around by
the wind. Do things need to be centered? Not—
 really, And there is also a quarterly effort to plant lilies,
lilies as far as the eye can see,   the
urban garden   on the   rooftop heralds
vertical tomatoes, rosemary, squash, and chives,
dill.   There is   preservation; and when
the   highways were erected above

*homes, above   our   heads, the sun
leaned more to the left.*
    *The lilies were erected around the freeway, to dis-
tract. The lilies are   allowed to be or they
    are forgiven. The lilies elicit emotion in the
politicians and in the citizens   who vote them
in. When we move as a collective, in unison, we think of it of
as fragile, tenuous, and this   landscape
urbanism, isn't it all a   transient thing?*
  *The vegetation, the horticulture, the sweating, we want
to know more. 'But Williams
is withholding, evading', they say. They talk so much shit. I'm
tired from the effort my body has made to   cho-
reograph.   My old   drawings, in
pencil, chalk. It looks a mess, the tracing paper,
shapes,   patterns, circles. We make   out
an oak leaf, the word,   oak. A circle set against a   line.
Texture, yes texture, that's important.
The iris against the dewdrop   grass,
against yarrow, the purple geraniums against the   sage,
    salvia, pink calyxes, lupine, acacia,
golden rod, aster (white and purple), and the brown-eyed
susan,   the*

ON THE FOREARM:

car breaks down. We try to get   back on the
road, but the coilovers, or the heating
pump, it needs coolant, we think. The boxes and bags are bent
    up in the trunk, squished   on
    the floor of the back seat. We take the ten CDs out of
the in-car entertainment system.   We
    don't have more provisions, see, we're stuck. Money is
running   low.   And we are   tired.
Bone   tired. We pull over, outside clothes, out of
gas, emptied, and   we stumble upon nothing, dirt,
and   we stumble upon the horses. We ride some
horses down   the valley. We slip in mud, spot
a UPS and we see to   the boxes, shipped right
    back, and the bags.
We   know our trip is almost over. We
don't   need the   items, see? Later,
when we meet   the   protest   it is
    already at its culmination, and   we
notice smoke,   there's some coughing
    going on due to the forest
fire blowing   our way, their way, horses
coughing, filled with   smoke, and we
stop to grab   some of the free
water bottles. How do I explain?   We spot the
    crowd.   We   dismount, we
tie the six   horses   up, up we
go, we give   the horses water   from
the plastic   water bottles.
And I'm   really   the one   who
knows how to tie   a horse up and how to lead them to water,
    the   others don't
really know how,   we're all   dehydrated,

and I find a post to tie them, the crowd is thick. Genocide, the crowd bemoans, I climb on stage. It is an unexpected thing, impromptu, unplanned, I simply step forward onto a makeshift stairway, some people help, I lean my full weight on top of them, I lean my sutured body over, and when I am carried forward, pushed or served up to the stage, to the microphone, I speak at length of phlox, and then of the white pine, of the types of trees that are in the air burning, orange, oak, I show the crowd how to move like smoke, this way and that, my arms in a port des bras. I mention black liberation, Tovex, C4, MOVE, move your ass, it's happening again, I say—most seem to agree, they nod their little heads, they watch the movement 'look at this old bag', they seem to say, singing, didn't my lord deliver Daniel?... we're singing about the upper way, planting feet on higher ground, floor work, the pain is ridiculous, I laugh, the subcutaneous sutures holding back the organs, or the non-absorbable staples, to keep me; though some are not so moved by the Spirit and walk away, or they snicker, pointing, and the rest are neutral. We see the girl, Matches, in the crowd. How has she arrived here? Has

she been   flying again? When I holler into the
       mic about the earth
       swallowing us   whole—Matches calls
out   my name, 'Vonetta!'—or when I discuss the
taste of the soil, acrid,   chunky, and
high   in nitrogen, or about how Alice
Walker's doctor told her as child, the eyes are
       sympathetic, what happens to one will also happen
to the other, sympathy, I repeat,
sympathy, the arm is   sympathetic I say to
the masses, going on about social action,
rough livability,   staying
quiet/   moving through destruction, or otherwise
       speaking up, [landscape design]. I
order   the crowd to be more predictable
in   their   coughing, cough cough,
remain stewards   of care!, I say. Matches is
       repulsed,   but one or two others
are untethered   by my word,   mark my
words, I say, and with this   prophecy we will know
the earth, though soon   enough I am
guided   down,   offstage, backstage,
       then down some   other set of stairs,
and then we are ready   to go back from whence
we came.   My lips   hurt (Janet)
my hips hurt, really,   there is
       dermatitis on the   legs, a red and
painful   swelling on the
shins,   hot to   the touch,
bruising. There is a dark mark above   the eyebrow, a
                                        discoloration
from a small kick on the   way out. The vitrectomy
was   successful, Seret and I with our
debris-free eyes, sympathy   in both eyes, but there is

also tingling down   in the feet, a
pain in the   ball
     of the foot, joint pain, a relevé, swelling in the
extremities. Osteopenia, weak
     knees. It is hard to walk almost at all.
Inflammatory.   The crowd helps me,
     down. And the suture is   breaking open
near the pubic   line and underneath. In the bed, we have
no saddle, our skin is raw and   the muscles in
our inner
     thighs ache. We have sold everything for these
horses,   the camera equipment was sold, though we
removed and preserved many   rolls of tape,
and hours   upon hours of footage. When the
sun finally goes we think it is wise to simply be   on
our way, or to
     move   along, move it,

SOLE OF THE FOOT:

*Bronco, not white like Orenthal's, but navy,
two door, manual transmission. A 1966,
perhaps a 1967; and while we slow
down and park on the shoulder, they record me sitting in the driver's seat, tight, eating fried
okra from a ziplock bag.
We're getting on. And when we drive slow, up the
mountain, or otherwise make wide turns through,
we enjoy it, we arrive at it. Grass stains on
knees. We brush our behinds off
The dirt sticking to us, the six of us squished
in. While heading straight for a long while
we push a CD into the Kenwood Electronics system
(accommodates ten CDs). A compilation,
something someone burned.
the bass comes in. There's limit-
ed skipping, covered in
rubber. Our place is receding or is
already gone. Behind, the fog is
low. The camera follows
our every move. Hand hanging out,
windshield wipers
going. Some boxes and bags rattling around in the back.
Keloids on our shoulder. When
the riots come we are on the road, we miss
them. We settle for a while in
Seattle. We talk some, we pass brit-
tlebush, sand verbena, lupine, primrose. Oh, talking about the
same shit but also about laughter
bursting forth, or the times we have tried to be more
composed, hold it together. I
begin, and it becomes a soliloquy,*

*a   a sermon, and the six
of us are taken with the view, so unlike our own. I
         command them as I gear   down (hum-
ming), looking between us,   and between the
driver's seat and the road, I say: in Mahogany,   Billy Dee
                            Williams (in the role of
Bryan) cannot hold it   together. Did you notice how he
        laughs in   a way that is endearing, private,
low, down   to the ground, while also failing
so thoroughly   to deliver   any   of his
lines? So Billy Dee says, 'Put one of these   buttons on,   okay?,' some   buttons made for a
political campaign, and then Diana Ross (as Tracey) shouts
out that   she is a widow from   the
South   Side, so Billy Dee responds 'ah, yes,'
and then, Diana goes on talking   about her old
man left her with six kids; she's messing around,
she's messing   with   him, 'the heat's
been off for a week,' she says, and   it's here   that
Billy Dee begins   to   laugh, Oh! He
looks down, toward that   unemployment   office floor, 'okay,' he laughs, as if
she is saying the silliest   thing, 'well,' he
says, and laughs some more, not holding it
together at all, no—'and   all the kids got the
flu,' Diana interrupts before he can get
another   word in, 'what are you gonna do
about   that?' Billy Dee, covering his mouth with his
left   hand, you know, barely trying, it's
clear, losing   all
         composure, 'well,' he says, 'have you spoken with your
landlord madam?' He   scratches
the back of his head. 'Landlord nothing,' she says, 'I want my
old   man   back!'*

*He's wearing a cream turtleneck, thick, a navy coat, a
mustache. And   what a nice
mustache. She wears a red dress with a black   neckline, a red shawl, or a   red kimono, a beige or
white   coat in her hands. And he is trying to
explain   what Diana should do   from the
authority of a city alderman, the office to which he soon
hopes to be elected. He's trying   to explain, he stammers,
'this heat issue is another,   matter altogether. Another... another', repeats it, and then he
laughs, flummoxed,   though   we do
not see   him laugh,   we hear it, the camera
on Diana/Tracey   and the   kimono/
shawl, a single   shot, her hair
coiffed, her most beautiful   teeth, the neck and eyes
         heavy. Covered up his lips   again, Billy
Dee, and this is where I   I realize.   They like each
other too much, off   camera,
there's   too much chemistry between them. He is
         smitten to the core ,
there's   something really   going on. And
when he laughs   Billy   Dee
         (whose real   name is William
December   Williams Jr.)
                 maybe he always covers   his
mouth like   that, December,   even
at   home with his   family, and he does it in the scene because it comes
natural   to him, when he is flummoxed or not holding   it together at all, at all, covering up
his   mouth   with the left hand. 'Have
you spoken with your (laugh), block association?
       Because,   because, you don't have a block
association in   on your street,*

do you? Do you?' This second asking, he's regaining some self-possession, or some equilibrium. I'm watching this movie and I'm thinking, are they just gonna allow them to do whatever the hell they want? They're riffing, laughing, fucking around. They're letting them play and fuck around. Listen, so Billy Dee goes on about how he can step up to meet the needs of the community, okay, and I think maybe he really could if he ever got the chance to do it, though we don't know if he ever will, or if he is successful in any way, even by the end we don't know, though he is charming. He looks good. And then I think, this character, Bryan, as played by December, his life will not be fortuitous or lucky, he will probably die young, a heart attack, though they don't show it. They go back and forth like that, and so on and so forth. But Diana wants to return to the issue of her old man, see, what will the potential alderman do to help her get her old man back? Because she sure does need her old man. She repeats this. Because Diana can't get along without her old man. Because they (the people sitting in the unemployment office) all need their old men, she emphasizes as she looks around, arms set wide and reaching toward them, them all. She is toying with him, and he is losing. Covering his forehead and his nose.

December is lost. Tracey/Diana knows

December wants to return to the issue of his position, and therefore back to the unemployment itself, aren't they all here to get some relief? So she cuts him a break, she says, 'and give me a job, you know what I mean?,' because he might be able to handle the question, she throws him a bone, that's one thing he can maybe speak to, as a future alderman, maybe he can speak to the job issue, she wants him to redeem himself, she's giving him a chance to show them, cramped up in this office, or to convey something of value to them, and the crowd has gathered around, they are erupting with glee, giddy, and here comes Billy Dee again, his hand, goddamn, covering his eyebrow again, his teeth, he laughs, and the whole of the improvisation has left him unmoored, shy, blushing, helpless, and covering everything up. The point of the film seems not to be about Diana choosing between personal success/career and a man (though the man is what she chooses in the end) nor is it about the man himself, maybe it's more about choosing companionship, choosing hope, or something? Or not choosing whiteness/eurocentrism. Will she ever design clothes again? Not if it interferes with Billy Dee's political aspirations, no. And I don't know that Diana/Tracey will be happy with him longterm, but of course, she runs home. She runs back to Chicago, is he a home? Is there no choice but to return ? Shit. It's romantic, if you like such things, in a straightforward way, and it is sad. You root for them, though we want her to to do her own thing, and after the heart attack maybe, or immediately after the credits run, just out of frame, we hope she'll go about her business without anyone at all. These men, these men, they use her up completely, in Rome and in Chicago, Norman Bates using her up, walking three steps ahead of her, as is custom, and then they give her the name Mahogany, 'mahogany,' I mean, it doesn't get any worse than that; and when she emerges from the crowd in the end talking about her old man again, there he is.

She will support his career in politics. Yes. Her old man. So again, maybe the call of the film is this: share your life, don't go at it alone? Or even, home is where the heart is! Return, not for happiness but for duty. It's only Diana Ross' second film, and she is the second child of six, and it also seems to me that at that time her career was at its peak, and not something Diana would have sacrificed for anyone, not something she would give up or quit, not for a man, though she quit the Supremes, and Berry was involved in all that, a handler... I don't suppose if it came right down to it that Diana would have chosen anything but herself, and her own five children... that interview she did with the lilac suit on? Whew, she looked real good. The interviewer mentions her energy, like, the great funk of her energy, or something, and attributes this energy or funkiness to her being a black woman, Diana's eyelids, she bats the hell out of those long eyelashes, false eyelashes on the top and on the bottom, the slightest hint of blue on the lids, red lipstick, the long red nails, the red silk collar, hair feathered, bouncing, gold hoop earrings, and that lilac suit! 'The world has not fucked me,' Diana says to the interviewer, and I agree. The world has not fucked me yet! Diana, all red and rained out in the park in 1983, the one spotlight pushing down, and the wind throwing the chiffon here and there, the red unitard. I was there in the front, and Mona was not yet born. The sky all grey. Soaked, blown, so she directs people to leave, Diana says, 'okay now, exit the park.' She says, 'is that a pistol in your pocket or are you glad to see me?' And in 'Mahogany,' when they leave the unemployment office, or when she travels to Rome and Billy Dee follows, okay, he is out of place. She is right, and he's wrong. He's wrong, he pouts, he judges the architecture, the wide streets, the sound of cars, and a scooter. In the foreground it's just the two of them. Tracey with the mink brown scarf around her neck, but otherwise monochromatic, black all over. Black hat, black shirt, black leather pants, a large black bag hanging at her knees. She looks good, she looks great. They walk through a   piazza, Bryan with his turtleneck,   dark this time. An aqua   blazer, with dark patches at the elbow. A good look, but he's not   in command. Is he ever in   command in this godforsaken film? I don't think so, I really don't think, though   some say he   regains control by the end, when she runs   back, but I disagree, he's not   in control.   There is a scene where he yells, but he's not   in charge, not ever. When he   fights the guy, Norman Bates, he seems to be   in control, but he's   not. Don't they fight over a gun? They've just come back from the tailor, and   they are meant to   look   different, elevated. They're not [in Chicago]   anymore, the   director wants us to note, they're not home, or in the ruins, okay?—They're not with   us, they're in 'utopia,' they're free, in that white   ass place they   hold   shopping bags with both   hands. And then, then, they enter   a   restaurant or a bar. Tracey/Diana speaks to the waiter. She is speaking in the language of the   place.   This is important, it's   big,   and there goes Billy   Dee/Bryan/ December covering his   mouth again,   unserious, breaking   character, because he cannot help himself. There is something he seems to find very   funny   about her focus on the foreign   language. He's here, visiting for the first   time,   this is her place, not his, hers, she's lived here for many months and she wants to show him.   Diana/Tracey speaking with the waiter, it begins with this,   'buongiorno signorina, che bello rivederla oggi,' and she repeats after him, 'rivederla oggi,' she stammers, it's just a greeting, an expression of pleasure in seeing another person again, even if it's disingenuous— a formality, and so Diana says, 'un bicchiere di vino bianco per favore'—suddenly the waiter loses his patience with her, 'what do you want lady, some wine?' he says. He switches to English. I'm watching this thing, and he doesn't give her a chance, even though she's doing quite well. She persists, 'si, si signore', and even though she's done quite well the waiter is exasperated with her, and I'm thinking, maybe he's tired, or perhaps something has happened to his wife, maybe she has the sugars, her foot amputated, and that is why his fuse is so short with this black woman, does he realize the cameras are rolling? And Diana's attempt is good, a valiant and respectable effort on her part. Can you imagine what December is doing during the exchange? Well, his head is bent all the way down into his hands, buried, doing the thing that he does, giggling, goddamn, 'okay fine' the waiter relents, while Diana/Tracey pushes on with a 'bene bene molto grazie, grazie,' pushes, she doesn't give up, moving into territories of the most calm, natural order, and Bryan loses it, cackles, busts out laughing, a release, 'that's heavy,' he says, and she is free to be ridiculous,

*or to find some small joy, though in a
few scenes this joy will be eliminated, no longer, but for now she is free to
order white wine in the language of the place,
oh, to sit in it, a sense
of ease, confidence, unafraid, for now, to stammer
along, or to be taken
at her word, in December*

GROIN:

a twin bed that can be moved into different   posi-
tions, adjusted for feedings, for changing.
Lifted or laid   down flat. Always plugged in.
And what can I say   about laughter,
what can I add   to the conversation about not
holding it   together? I've experienced
that. I hear laughter coming   from the living
*   room, or from the kitchen. And*
there's that tale about daddy, we know how
Obit used to be sick and then be   well,
a person with all kinds of   ailments,
disease,   and how he   would die
every day, every single day, a   death. But he
went forward   to meet   it with
glee, he approached this horror with pleasure, or with
*   abandon, he would*
*   laugh and laugh, Obie, Obie Williams, used to call*
him Obit, wouldn't   he die every   day?
Collecting   his own   obituaries like
a sport,
*   loud, raucous,   ridiculous, though they*
say it was a grift,   a performance, or that he
pretended to   die
but no I watched him do it, we watched   him get
through all the pain of it, the daily   pain, the daily
death, and the fear,   of   dying
every single   day, a   fear which
never   diminished though he would come to know
*   its sensation well. The   feeling of it*
approaching, 'it feels like   falling,' he told
me, too   early, 'or like   flying,' And
wouldn't he laugh and laugh,   and laugh if

*you caught him on the way
to the place where he would soon perish, he was open
with delight, delightful. We already know about it.
Drowned, stabbed, and that one time he
fell, blood from the head, when he was
climbing the asphalt and hit his
head on the sidewalk, and it split open like a
watermelon. Little seeds burst
forth from the opening. The blood dripping, splashing us all. It got on my shirt, and on the
sidewalk the blood was very red, thick, burgundy,
and black. I took him up,
I picked up the seeds. I buried him. I plated him. The time he
had the heart attack, just out of frame, leg
amputated, Mona in
the backseat, Mona in the back
laid out and quiet on leather.
'You drive too slowly,' she says, and it's true we
were hours behind schedule. My eyes
were not so good anymore, I could not
drive at night, for example, with
my stomach protruding
bouncing against the steering wheel, they
thought my water might break
the way the contractions were coming.
    Mona is close to sleep,
Sanaa is on her phone, checking on the
child and the sitter. Jackie is counting the
odds, biting her nails, Beryl is doing the cross-
word. I begin my criticism of 'Love
Jones,' mostly to myself, the others are focused on their
things, on their sleeping, or
their mothering. I mutter under
my breath and begin with this: the*

dangers of riding a motorcycle without a helmet. Lathan rolls her eyes and says nothing. For the rest, I thought it brilliant, I say, or that it was the most subtle and complex depiction of black friendship. Mona moans a 'no' from the back, she's awake but feeling rather lazy. Sanaa doesn't interrupt. Haven't y'all noticed the dynamic between the tertiary characters, and the way of the dialogue? Or the lighting of their skin? And Seret says, At school we would watch 'Love Jones,' three, four times a week, often enough to know it by heart, five. Or even

  'Five on the Black Hand Side,'
  'Shaft,'
  'The Wiz,'
  'Thomasine & Bushrod,'
  'Losing Ground,'
  'Drylongso,'
  'Hoop Dreams,'

part of the school curriculum, she said. We created the curriculum ourselves. And though the government has recommended the one film about a man and a woman and another woman who are stranded at sea, 'Orchard Beach,' Seret says, after a while we grew bored with it— Nina on the back of the bike with no helmet, the roads all slick. We see Nina, on the back of a

motorcycle, no helmet.   *'Give me my propers,' Seret says,*
I cracked   *my*   *pelvis once, broke*
              both   *wrists falling from a*
bike, a bike, a bike.   *When that man picked*
me   *up from the school*
grounds, and when he tried to pick me up from the ground
               after the fall, the break, to gather
me   *from the asphalt, pulling me up by the hips,*
I   *told him to quit it, 'just leave me*   *down*
here,' I said 'just leave me here until the medics
come,'   *'call the*   *medics,' and while I was*
waiting for the ambulance, down, not moving, not even an
        inch, I   *thought about the way Darius*
says, 'oh yeah, I got   *your number,' cocky,*
barely   *holding*   *in his*   *thrill, and how*
it cuts abruptly to the motorcycle,   *we're*
          behind them, unhelmeted,   *and*
her hair moves so pretty in the wind. And though I
understand   *Nina's*   *omis-*
sion, we cannot shame her   *recklessness,*
    the way she's on the bike,   *I*
understand that Illinois has no   *helmet law,*
though they do require goggles or a windshield, her perfectly
bowed legs wrapped around   *metal, the*
waiting, she can't bear   *the metal, metal, metal*
of waiting—   *and Sanaa*
Latham puts her   *phone down to say, 'it's Josie*
                       that I   *love,*
not   *Nina, and it's Josie's teeth that I like, the*
gap, her lips, the way   *she*   *sits*
in the cab, shoulders squared and facing her friend, she is
    direct, she stares   *her*
down.' When Nina looks away in an attempt to hold it, just for
a second, Josie says, 'you   *fucked him*

*didn't you?', and Nina bursts open, looking
down, nodding,   and Josie
    continues, 'and you weren't even gonna
tell me?' the cab driver is listening in,
    and the way Josie looks at Nina, with
longing, with   intrigue, or in a knowing way,
she   knows, pulling,
'you ain't   slick, you can't
    keep that kind of shit from   me!' she says.
Josie understands,   the scene
    mostly   improvised and the shot
was hard for the cinematographer to   get, the
back   and forth,   two cameras,
the most thrilling, open   way,   fucking on the   first   date, which
I've practiced many a time, and how she slips
and falls on his dick, and then they get into the girth, Darius,
'it was like his   dick   just
talked to me.'   'What it say?'—look at
the chemistry! This is chemistry, look   at
the way they face each other; fine, good,   solid,
curious.*

          *We
get off   the   I-95S, to the
bridge, to I-80W, we keep left at the fork, we keep right at
    the fork, take   Exit 21, and then we
    continue on to US-20W, US-75S, merge
onto   I-29N, I-90W, stay on until
Exit 2C for I-5N. When we leave
    Mona on the side   of the road, it
is quick, and I catch   her sleepy face: lost
and   wet, in the side mirror she is on her
knees, shifting around in the dirt. And when   we turn
around to pick   her up again, she is sitting on*

her   side, waiting and bereft.
Palms the color of   mace, the lacy membrane derived
from around the nutmeg   seed.
Nutmeg is the seed. She gets back in on the right side, leg
*   in the air,   stretching, she climbs,*
she curses   us out. She falls asleep. When we
stop   for gas   we are still
*   laughing. To move our bowels, to shit, or to take a*
break, to stretch. The   smell was dirt,   we
*   stank to high   heaven. We pass the*
*   roundabout. We die*
*   laughing. The group of us, we think we*
*   know it   all. We   argue, six. I know a little*
about   soil, deposits, leaves. I tell them
about soil,   deposits, leaves.   Seret
knows about a man   like   Darius,
*   'though his name was Darnell', she says, and the way*
he picked   her up on his bike was the   same,
just   like Darius picks   up
Nina, though in the film they do   not fall
down at all, and Seret and Darnell fell almost
immediately, they   fell   down
in the rightmost   lane of the street, and Darius
and   Nina didn't, they   kept on. 'Oh
yeah   I got your   number,'
Darnell said to Seret while she was   down
on the asphalt, the   raised asphalt, pelvis
cracked, he meant only that he saw   her, she says, or
knew something   about her, 'knew my character,'
she says, and she couldn't focus   on the insult because the
pain was   excruciating, and   so he
picked up the bike, spotless,   undamaged,
and waited   somewhere nearby, nearby and
behind,   and he was just out of her line of

*vision,   she could only see the many tires   of the
cars that were   moving past
      so slowly, the large wheels of the bus moving
      past her misshapen body, she created so
much   traffic.*

                              *When we reached the
coast, the water spilled   over, broken. Waters
      raised up on its hind legs, something wet on my
hands. The cloth   seats soaked through. We
ignored it for a   while, to discuss the way Lena
Horne smiles on the 1974 cover   of
Ebony magazine, red, or the way her mouth is open real
wide, we moved to Janet   Jackson
and the way she laughs on 'Got 'Til It's Gone,' and Sanaa
wants to reference the way   Thomasine and
Bushrod laugh after the first bank robbery, and Mona wants
to consider Zora   Neale Hurston   and
Langston's use   of laughter in 'Mule Bone.' Mona
says,   'Hurston and   Hughes   both
considered   laughter to be one of the foremost
         characteristics   of black peo-
ple. It is captured in their collaboration Mule Bone,' she
says—we only cut her off   because the fluid*

                                                          *is all

over us. We are   obnoxious, wet, and
tired, and we cannot think   straight, we turn
     the car towards the exit, and I'm
thinking how cruel it is to   pretend to leave
someone   behind   in the
middle of   the road, even if we did apologize,
sorry sorry   sorry. I   drive myself
to   the hospital, laborious. I'm the
only one with a valid   license. Seret
cuts   in when   I'm*

laying on my back, saying something about how
Janet   laughs   soft, do you feel
*   that?, Kamaal asks her, she's in the booth, a   place*
of labor,   and she laughs, ha   ha ha, three
*   notes, reaching that octave, or*
a high pitched   noise/sound, a pause, and then
another ha   ha ha ha ha, eight total, so   we
assume that she   feels

ON THE LACE OF BOTH WRISTS:

contraction comes. The contraction comes without
contrition, but with a wave or a blow.
There is   a sharp pain in the arm, the abdomen
splits, split   muscle, and near the elbow, or
*   something waiting to blow. A splitting migraine. I*
cannot see any figure,   blurry.   A
spitting image—the contractions come, blown. What is a
Braxton   Hicks? Straight   lines
*   tattooed upon a black arm. Diana   Ross*
red and rained out on the small   television.
Hung   high and in the corner. 'If there's a cure for
this, I don't,'   the teenagers
say or   sing in   unison. The teenagers
are invading my space.   Keys
under the welcome mat, we pick   them up, click
them in, we turn   the knob, I hear them
whisper, sing-song-like.   The house is spotless, it is as I left
*   it. I   know it from its empty sound.*
White sage, incense, and   lavender. The persis-
tence   of gold or silver on our hands,
these young   hands are using a wash
cloth behind my   neck, under the arm pit. 'Look
back   at it', somebody can be heard   yell-
ing through an   open window. Central; the press of the
backpack cutting   into the
*   teenage shoulders. The press of the washcloth on the*
shoulder blade. They remove it. They sit close
to my face. Breathing all in my face, smelling of musk and
*   chewing gum, milk. 'Coming   back*
is   disorienting,' I try to tell them. I
make the lights go on and off. Our stuff
returned   here, shipped

back, this was not the plan. 'What?' someone says, 'Yeah, yeah.' And another says, 'we did not have enough provisions, no food, no gas, and money was tight.' 'That's right,' I say. I try to nod my head. The adults boss the teenagers around. To return home— wrong? Has anyone noticed our short absence? Packed up or in storage or in the back of the car? On a horse bareback? Diana Ross under the welcome mat, red, there's rain coming down. We've run out of gold. Gold bars sitting in the backpack, gold grills. My mother, the hem of her heavy skirts, hair twisted this way and that, bruising, hitting her neckline. I don't know where my mother is. The man is gone, there will be no more talk of him. Incarcerated, gone. Lost in the system, we think. We haven't heard from him, and later we find out that he was released, held for a day or two, tortured and then released, months ago, after all the looting and the fires, the self-immolation, rioting, rolling blackouts. Probationary. We do not see him again. There is a change, the women, the roommates, mass graves, now alone, alone in the sense that we are rid of things, dead, like Burle— though he did not commit any crime, none at all, innocent—and he was incarcerated to demolish, he has always been good at finding the exit.

The baby comes and goes. 'Yes', I say. Water broken in a dream. We think he goes about his business. We don't say anything. We don't bring it up. Gunn. On the major Holiday we pile one on top of the other; some neighbors still send their congratulations, congrats, congrats, congrats, 'Is he coming?' Mind you, the belly protrudes. In a dream I watch the film. Tradition, sedition; put into the system. The footage is still going in the living room, will it ever end? Someone singing. Seret's voice— 'Haven't I learned all that I can? Haven't I been picked up at the waist, dropped off, felt/filled up, yolked up, gathered, jerked, man-handled?' 'Be more discreet,' I want to say. Relax your shoulders. Painting my toenails red. I am emptied, an adjustment. Laying their sharp tongues within the groove of my stretch marks. I am deflated, groovy, weak. 'What age is she now? 319?' The contractions coming in a few minutes apart, bloodying up the sheets. And in a whisper someone says, 'sometimes, we die/cry.' We perform the breathing exercises, feel him kicking. 'Vonetta! is not really among us,' they say. 'Vonetta! is unlucky.' I move closer to childhood. Seret moves closer to child hood, or she regresses. I want to be mothered. There's an opening left and I take it. To be perpetually mothered. My

*mother's bangles clanging. 'Yes', they say, her long experience
    with a womb. I gravitate toward the smothering.
They wipe the backs of my knee—'especially since she
is hard   to the touch, the baby walked right out
    of the hospital room,'   the
neighbors say. A clear broth with mushrooms, six
doubles on the side, tamarind sauce,   I smell the lilies on   her   breath. Older
in her thinking, though her   hips are   fresh.
Tingle,   tingle. Tingling all   over.
She is   new   to me.
There is some   newfound
respect. She helps   me with the soil
    in the   courtyard, soil on feder-
al land, 'we have   no business   tending to it,'
the government says.   We walk
    there and   back,
and bending down, or sowing   the land,
watering, such bitterness,   such bitter
soil, it tastes real chalky, is that
good?   of liberty, let it resound.
    Everything has been
unpacked, put back in its   place. I   like the shape
    of her teeth. A small mouth, how I
watch it. Bouncing breasts, titties   out.
Do we have the surveillance   clearance?
She's   in charge of the   children.
We get along, though some of us   are dying
off. I begin   washing
    the floors, 'The   Secret Life of Plants'
playing. 'Ain't But The One Way' playing.
      I wash   the surfaces,
the mahogany   stranded at sea.   Someone
braids it, parts it. They do not remove the fingers. I'm nestled*

between her legs. I'm in between, she
    wants to braid my hair every other day (not on
weekends, and not on the
Wednesday).   *'The weekends aren't meant for*
labor', she says, 'the weekend is for [illegible],'
    tilling the earth like labor to me,
pushing, and we drive on, to the middle, which
    takes approximately forty-nine hours
there and back. Not cooped up, we
    take the elevator, we leave at sunrise,
sometimes it is nothing. A man or two
    never come, a woman or two, no one, just us, There's
no time for it, no need to break
    the silence. 'Vonetta!' Diana Ross calls out. The film
    going on and on—there is no point,
    moving the leg into a grand battement.
We use our roses, and that is that. A lateral T, a stag.
90 degrees. 'There is nothing I hate
more than the fullness. Or to feel so
utterly bereft, left behind in everything grown.
There's too much youth in me,' Seret
says. The men don't come, nor do the
women. Low lung capacity, one lung left. Fill
my lung like a balloon. The sounds
from down the hall are grown; don't
    talk to the feds; and
they take their time, shell the peas,
wash the greens in the sink, horseradish
on the cuff. I am the one
    to do the bidding. I was the one. I enact
    the small labors.
Bring the grown sounds over from next door. She
sits with us. She moves in the bed.
The sound of us gathering is guttural.

*Matches fathering   seed.   Do you feel
that,   ha ha ha,   ha ha ha ha ha,
eight, so we know   that she feels it. 'The long   hours
     are nothing,'   down to
22,000, or so.   Bottom
     heavy, or how to tailor   a pant.
Being driven,   being   chauffeured,
or   going out for a case
of mangoes.   Someone moving in the front
room. Our   bottom   teeth
     showing. Larenz   is a name   for a
god, this is the last   thing I'll say
     about   gods, 'Vonetta!' I   know
about   fertilizer.   I got   your
     number, or a plate breaking in   two.
The footage   has been
edited,   put into the earth, placed in
     wood,   mahogany, the soil
in her finished   mouth,   burned, placed
neatly in the turn, I   mumble, the
water spilling, sprucing, the cloth seats soaking wet.
We saw   her give birth that   first
time, 60 years ago? 100? Tell anyone who will listen about
the   time   she
     was cut open like a wedding   cake.
What   she bore   was   akin
to a bird!*

PART III, *the film continued*

AN UNCEREMONIOUS EXIT.

The man pulls on his boxers. He gathers the fresh laundry and puts it to his nose. He has always loved the scent. It's already been folded up for him and pressed. His hair isn't lined up at all, he'll need to call on his barber. He rushes out, *gum beater* she calls after him. *Blowhard*—just before he slams the front door shut he meets Mo's eyes. And before that, prior to the name calling and the unceremonious exit, gathering the fruit from the kitchen, a mango, with the mango in hand tripping, stumbling over some camera equipment. When he gathered himself again he looked down to see if Mo had noticed the way his ankle turned over, rolled over like a doll in a child's hand, or the way he placed his palm on the carpet to steady himself.

Disgust on her face?

He looked down and over to the left, he saw the plastic couch left empty, sticky, and the eyes staring up from the floor, that clean carpet, the teapot hissing and hitting a wild note.

CHICKEN BONES.

The man, Burle, is known. To the mother, and to the waiting child, who grows slowly. Burle is known to the neighbors.

The friendship between Burle and the mother (henceforth Vonetta!) isn't strange, it just is. They've known each other. And between Mona and the mother there is glue, there is care, even with the forty years between them, seventy?

Don't call me the mother, she pleads.

Between Mona and Burle there is something about convenience, or an exchange. They're engaged to be married, though it isn't romantic, it's just an agreement for health insurance purposes, for the benefits, and between Vonetta! and Burle it is a familiar and nostalgic thing.

They're just waiting on the child to come, that's all, the neighbors say about the pair.

And as neighbors, we witness these people's lives through the windows, or we listen through the walls, we watch the film.

Sometimes we enter Von's apartment with the spare key; or we enter Mona's apartment without any key at all, since Mona always leaves the door unlocked, and sometimes this is how we witness the dysfunction/harmony of their home.

Sanaa Lathan lets herself in to rest while Lira watches a movie. Or to practice her sides. She lays her child on the carpeted floor. Others listen in if they want to be nosey, from the doorways, the keyhole, they knock, they opt in or out, depending.

The lot of us, when we visit, bring something along. We never come empty handed: some bone broth for Vonetta! (for the health of her bones, to replenish the collagen, and for the baby).

This is how we perceive them—up close. An arm, a quadricep. Otherwise things are perceived from afar. Vonetta! fixing up some griddle cakes for Burle. Mona slamming the front door, or yelling in the hallway, *spoiled thing*, or yelling while waiting for the elevator to reach.

A gasp or a pounding. Burle laughing behind her, *hard hard hard*, from the gut.

Burle is sometimes alone in the women's apartment. He'll grab something out of the fridge, a snack, a piece of fruit, a mango, the pressed underwear, and leave before he is spotted. He moves downstairs.

Vonetta! passes him on her way up. She says, *Burle*, and keeps on. He looks at the belly, says nothing.

Burle watches Von! from downstairs and across the street. He thinks about her from downstairs and across the street. He thinks about how back in the day they used to be on the verge of violence.

Violent in a good way!, he says, though we can't imagine how that could be.

The wind is picking up, we're cold and undecided. What a face he has. Symmetrical, the long nose. Burle tells the story, how back then they would not give each other space, the pair of them, *tied*, he says, *that was the violence of it. We were stuck at the hip. Isn't it violent, to be so close? To have no breathing room? I always had too much space as a child, my parents didn't see to me or tend to me, I was always given too much space. Vonetta! didn't give me any space*, Burle smiles, *she didn't let me breathe. It felt like care. It felt like care at the time. A mothering.*

He mumbles something about the child in utero, he thinks about the child changing or shifting, suffering, we can't quite pick it up.

It's important to note that something imperceptible is

shifting in the mother too, it's not just the child, it's Vonetta! too. And we agree, we see it in the way she unpacks her shit. The way she hunches over, curved like hell, or the way she stares into space. Her body clicking, snapping, her knees shot. The trip west was not successful, and that's part of the loss, we think. The way Vonetta! leans down into the boxes, the way she pulls the scotch tape from them, all rough, all violent.

Vonetta!/Burle are done thinking that they owe each other a thing.

We ask them, *do you owe anything?* And they say *no, nope.*

In their knowledge of the way they used to be, there is certain paranoia/obsession/simultaneity. Burle thinks he will be a good father when the time comes. He thinks he will be ready, whenever it comes, in a few months, in ten years—he has never before had the opportunity.

They've picked up their old habit of nagging, picking, playing.

Someone did set the building on fire, Burle tells Bobby while sitting on Vonetta!'s couch on the Friday, a day of splitting—*everyone rushed down the water was coming out the fire hydrants and Matches poor Matches she picked up her skirt and flew straight up out of there. She flew! I'm telling you. An ascension. Picked up her skirts and moved up above us. Flew all the way south with the waterfowl. Saw her go straight through a cloud yes indeed. And was she in on it? We don't know. All the files burned up all the school records. And then there was another fire the next day and the day after. There was a fire today down at the city hall. They're going to burn us all down down down we're going to expire.*

They're calling for Matches to sacrifice a limb any limb or they want to present her with a fine for the water damage imagine a teen, a fifteen-year-old girl! They want her to repent! Shit. So if she decided to burn something down after all can we blame her? If her name is a prophecy can we blame her?

It was the blood from his head that had acquainted us, Vonetta! explains. *That young man, he was young once, Burle, short, lanky, climbing the asphalt in the heat, he fell and hit his head on the sidewalk. It split open like a melon.*

Little seeds burst out from his open head. The blood dripping, splashing us both. It got on my shirt, and on the sidewalk the blood was very red, thick, burgundy, and black. I took him up, I picked up the seeds. A stranger, I took him. I bandaged him, I swallowed a seed, I held his head together with the heel of my hand. My sister, Simona, was not yet born. And when I removed the plastic tabs from the skin toned Band-Aids (which did not match our own skin tones) Burle let out a moan.

I sewed his ass up. He went to leave, all fixed up, sutured, with a salve on his skin made from tea tree oil, honey, lavender, garlic, ginger, the gauze and the tape and the white people band-aids, and when he got up to leave he got tripped up again, right over his own legs, a clumsy bastard.

I sat on a plastic covering set over a brown couch.

Burle gathered himself and was close to the doorway when he fell again, against the baby grand piano, and we both became anxious about his instability, his inability to balance, was he concussed? Hit his knee, it happened in the span of minutes: a fall outside, boom, right on the head and then another fall against the piano stool.

What a clumsy, clumsy man, Vonetta! said. She checked his knees. The peroxide was put back on the shelf and the other materials went into the medicine cabinet.

She asked him, *do you need the doctor?* He said, *no, no. Okay, okay then*, she said. He thanked her and left his number, limping, *bye bye*, he said, slamming the door behind him.

The man was upon her. He entered the room in time,

or he had returned, knocking on the door, *tap tap tap,* Vonetta! allowed him back in.

Her back was bare, she bent and the rolls moved. The pockets of the mother's body were folded, *not yet a mother.* He squeezed them. He bit her shoulder. And it is only his elbow upon her thigh.

The neighbors were listening then just as they continue their listening now—*We seen a nose from the window frame, since the beginning of time we've seen it—an elbow upon a thing, bags under the eyes, hair follicles or something with hair. We hear a shout, a thump. And they seem like a cliché when they do it, this pair, for they become a blur. These young things, they could not be told apart; they are ravenous and indecipherable, paranoid, simultaneously engaged—*

Sanaa Lathan denies it, when she hears the neighbors tell it she says, *no, no.*

There is an unfamiliarity setting in, an anxious energy. And the neighbors insist, *we know fast-thing, that fast Williams girl, we know it's her window, her mother, Nora, out working two jobs, Obit not working but dying continuously, three, and we sure enough know the individual, the boy, Burle, and his wide shoulders.*

There is a child between them—*is he coming?*, people ask.

No one knows. Has she been with child all this time? Forty, fifty, sixty years? *Maybe, maybe.*

Mona listens to the mother and the man before she leaves for work. The pair chat about something she doesn't understand, an inside joke from their time, something about Don Cornelius. She thinks about having a child, that wondrous thing, the aesthetic of it.

And when the man exits the backroom, he is still talking up a storm, directing his attention to Vonetta!. His demeanor is disheveled, and his hairline needs tending.

There are lines from the pillowcase on his forehead and on his arms there are scratch marks.

When talking, communing, why must these two be close to touching?

He takes a mango from the counter in the white kitchen. When he is tired of their company, these sisters, the man leaves, and Mona likes the way he closes the door, slamming it.

The ring of the elevator. The faucet running in the bathroom.

Mona is eating in the kitchen, or she is out of frame, near the window. Either way, she stands up, she stands and moves away, to eat and to think, like a soldier is forced to stand, or a dancer sometimes stands, shoulders down, neck extended, *unless the choreography calls for some other way, a curvature*, and she is overwhelmed with despair.

A few minutes after he leaves, *five or ten minutes after, depending*, the man can be seen from the window, he's down in the street, and nothing of the lines on his arms or the marks from the mother's pillowcase can be seen. Nothing of the long nails that have scratched him and drawn blood.

On Friday, everyone is split, separate, doing their own things.

Mona knows it's him, of course, because he stands on the street leaning with one shoulder down, one shoulder raised, uneven, and he stands in a spot near a blue tent that can be seen from the window, near the charred city hall he stands in a way that is thoroughly familiar. Mona doesn't have the vocabulary to explain this familiarity, but it is so.

Mona can sometimes be seen standing at the window from the spot below.

The man sees Mo in the living room window with the

most impeccable posture, the little teeth like pieces of gum, and he sees Vonetta! in the backroom window, and the pregnancy that is too full, the body almost breaking/ hips cracking.

The mother tells Mona many times over that the man from downstairs is her friend. *Friends. Just, friends. An old friend, a peer.*

Mona realizes quickly how mothers are, the way her own mother was, her mother that slept with a married man, Obit, and how Vonetta! is, and that mothers aren't frank about much, especially not themselves.

Burle is like a child, wild, unruly.

Has he ever listened to a word a woman has said?

He goes on and on about Matches, her flight, *can we fault that poor little winged thing?*

Mona understands their arrangement. She hires a wedding planner. They watch the Holiday footage together, or even the film with three people swimming without restraint in the sea. He likes the sea, just as she likes it. They watch it with child-like enthusiasm.

On the thick television: the water's expanse, the actress who mothers the other actress, a definitive hopelessness underlying them all, and a man, Billy Dee Williams, with the same facial hair as Mona's father, and Von's father. *I would like to have children*, Mona decides.

Then she gathers him up, Mona's long legs wrapped around Burle's waist and he is calm again. Mona is but twenty and two years of age, or something like it, or twenty-five, six, seven, nine or something, and her legs are longer than a mountain. Her arms too. The two sisters are so tall.

Mona is disastrously tall, Burle says, *a giant*, and Burle's lower back has begun to suffer from the weight of her upon him.

Mona climbs down, strips, and takes her place at the window.

Burle watches Mo from outside, from downstairs and across the street. Their intimacy is on the verge of silence. Mona is changing, suffering. Even after gifting her an endless supply of mango, it is obvious that something imperceptible is shifting in her. A certain paranoia, obsession or jealousy, impatience. Her lips are dark on the perimeter, pink where they meet in the middle.

Across the street and below, the man is looking up.

He watches Vonetta! lean to the right as she gathers herself in her hands. He watches Mona lean to the left for the mango. *Disastrous*, that was the word the man, Burle, had used to describe the circumstances. She had kicked his sorry ass out.

Disastrous?, the four syllables, with her wrists bruised up from all the rope. When Mona lets him in she's easy to fold, soft.

He waves at them both.

THE COMMNUNITY CENTER.

The community center is located in a glass building, the seats set up like an airport, bolted into the floor, some of them facing the others, and with one row set directly behind, while the rest are facing away/out/east.

LANDSCAPING.

Vonetta! Amethyst Williams' landscape designs still withstand. They live, though they shift every few hours, or every few days, every quarter hour, and then they dry out or are overridden.

The flora withstand for very little. From the window high up Vonetta! Amethyst Williams sees the remains of her work, the remnants of an evolving architecture of plant life. *And can plants be architecture? Can they exist in reverence the way the castles still stand, broken?*, the crew asks.

She thinks *yes, yes. But the more the landscape is lost to the aggressive seasonality the more it is ignored*, she says, *it cannot be a known structure, the Apollo.*

Vonetta! has lost the landscaping job, *0.4% of landscape architects are black*, she says.

In other words, she wasn't missed. In other words, or in turn, she has lost the ability to design upon existing spaces, or to choose native plants, or to choose from the county's still vibrant foliage—the weeds, thistle, grasses, mosses and the fungi, cactus, orchids, sunflowers, the cherry trees, ribwort plantain.

There is plant death all over; and for her to lose the authority to replant things or to make public spaces feel new/alive, but also familiar and nostalgic—to not do it, to be unable to do it, *it is a death, okay, to be employed is a sort of death, a death of self, and to be unemployed is also a particular kind of death, is it not?*, she says, *and to stop resourcing the plants, those that survive in the most extreme of weather? Isn't it a dying event?*

Vonetta! is unemployed.

A medium shot of her face, lines near her mouth and around her eyes. On the forehead, three lines. She's almost done unpacking her belongings. It is taking long, but she has completed the bulk of it, the lamps, the lampshade, the hat boxes, the herringbone suit, the painting of a woman, the painting of a girl, the poster of her mother, the painting of a man, all the figurative paintings, the ceramics, the family albums.

Vonetta! can see her professional efforts from the window. *And plants are better than a building can ever hope to be*, she says, *better because the buildings split or die, and the landscape splits only if tempted. Synthetic or natural grasses marked by the Clegg Hammer, checking for density, the depth of the infill.*

The plants bloom in quick succession, blooming and falling/failing repeatedly. It is not so striking for a neighbor to see something bloom over and over, or fall/fail in this quick succession. And for Vonetta! Amethyst Williams the change isn't upsetting. *It is real/enthralling!, or it makes all the sense in the world. Work with the existing ecology*, she says, *fell the tree, the root systems of white pine. Red pine, lilac, rosa rugosa.*

An untended garden can still bring her to tears, or bring her down to her knees, break her eardrum, and it happens especially when she stumbles upon the remains of her own delicate work while out for a short walk, and with her full belly poking, her organs pushed to the side, twisted, liver shifted irreparably and to the point of no return. Hair as white as milk.

The floods return to the wetlands.

And on those short walks when she encounters her own work, with the child kicking, skin distended, the emotion hits her and brings her down to her knees. And her knees bleed in the summer, and they do not bleed in the winter, for in the winter her knees are covered in wool, denim, leather.

I am so affected/afflicted by the ingenuity of the design, you see, of my own design, the ones drawn by hand on thick set cream paper, and by the geometry of the flowers blooming in a very determinate shape, so much so that my knees give out if I happen upon it, and if it's summer and I have on a short, breathable item my knees are left scratched and bleeding.

What Vonetta! Amethyst Williams did as the head urban landscape architect (henceforth: the architect) was to create something that spoke to lateness. She is late. Always late, in her designs and in her demeanor.

This explains why the work she's forged so far isn't beautiful. There is no emphasis on beauty in her practice. *Certainly if the beauty comes it is welcome, but it is not a priority.* She keeps the soil as it is. She uses fish and seaweed compost. She keeps the topography as it is, she plants around the boulders. Or she pulls everything out, and begins anew. We see it and it's quite plain. *It is not a priority for the space to be functional.*

What the architect wants most of all is circulation, the children say. *If the plan covers what was once a landfill, good. But the focus is not environmental in the slightest. It is about restraint, flexibility, proportion or time. What is the hierarchy? The spaces the architect creates are not recreational, but they exist, and they most certainly are not flood-resilient. She is renowned for her herbaceous flower borders,* the children say.

Land in disuse unintentionally made whole, if not a little dangerous, that's her thing. Yellow forsythia. She won awards of every order. The SSLA revealed her work to be a winner across all categories. It is rumored that the architect buried small personal items into the earth of her projects, and nothing that was planted was edible or sustainable.

When the highways were erected above the homes on the outskirts of the Hill, the sun leaned over everything except for us, the people, the architect says, *we got almost no sun and were made to go up to the rooftop.*

It's the way she is able to know, the children sing, *(and to know it intuitively) how a landscape will evolve over time, the natural change of it, an evolution. What is now green, will turn yellow in ___ years, or in ____ months, pastels, yellow, set against that native plant, the perennials, the annuals, purple.*

THE PLASTIC AND THE GUNS.

The plastic is sticking to Vonetta!'s legs and to Vonetta!'s fingers. We rewind to see. The white couch, ornate, but covered completely in plastic. *It's an expensive couch, bought at one time or another by a relative,* she tells us.

Vonetta!'s suprasternal notch, her jugular notch is saturated, with sweat moving down the bridge of her nose. On the plastic couch with her feet up, sweating, her thighs sticking, with the pink slingback heels on the feet, and her orange shower cap with the elastic perimeter; and underneath: extra virgin olive oil, mayonnaise, apple cider vinegar, an avocado, all things a relative had mentioned would help the hair become more supple.

Outside, snow. It covers the street, flat and clean.

She sits high up, on the second-highest floor of the apartment building. She doesn't budge from the place where she is sitting. She sits near the window, on the couch. Vonetta! can see the man, Burle, outside and far below, dressed in a dark color, perhaps a navy. We cut back and forth between them. Mona is gone, working.

He is so far from the white couch, so far down, minuscule, puny. He seems to be looking at the geese, or some other winged animal, and it is clear that his fists are clenched and supporting his chin, his knuckles sitting under his chin, folding, *folded skin.* The whites of his eyes are visible, not the pupils, but the whites. He is sitting.

Vonetta! believes she can make out the ripples in the chin, *look at the ripples,* she says, and there is a shadow there, underneath, and we see his neck and the full mouth all squished up against the knuckles.

The heat isn't up high, it's the hyperhidrosis that makes Vonetta! sweat through her clothing, her socks, between her toes, and from the bridge of her nose down to her lip.

Under her breasts. Outside the weather has turned again, a frigid Saturday. The Holiday is almost up.

The window is open, the noise carries. Vonetta! uses Johnson & Johnson baby powder, so the inner thighs are covered in the chalk, the cuticles and the lower abdomen are covered in this white powder. The breasts are covered.

Vonetta! has stopped using the talc-based powder, she uses the cornstarch-based powder, *they tell us,* she says, *that this new version is clean and does not cause any ovarian cancers.* Delicate rings on eight fingers, with the two empty thumbs. Gold rings, nails so long, so very long, with fresh flowers pressed into the acrylic, and when Vonetta! turns her palms up (as if in prayer) her natural nails appear shorter and yellowed underneath. Her cuticles are cut down, even though she knows it's bad, she has been told by a relative, *the cuticles should be pushed back, never cut down, it can lead to infection.*

She listens to the radio, a sermon about the power of Jesus.

She moves to change the station, but changes her mind. She loosens up... *it's soft, it's soft, you see.* Moving to something about Jesus, oh, about how Jesus is all forgiving, *we must count on Jesus,* the radio station says, *you must count on Him, you must forgive even if you are betrayed! Turn the other cheek.*

The blinds are bleached from the sun, crooked and waiting to conceal. She sits. The coconut oil has hardened on the sill. With her shirt tied up in a knot at her center, Vonetta! counts the loose bills: *twenty, thirty*, licking her fingers, *forty, forty-five, fifty, sixty-six, sixty-six, sixty-seven.* It isn't enough.

I don't feel like it, she says.

She doesn't want to do a thing. She doesn't want to finish unpacking her belongings. Undoing, or re-settling in.

Someone is crying, howling.

She thinks about the landscape, that odd, dry landscape [cut to flora of the west]. *Why must we always return?*—while underneath the radio proclaims—*home, Jesus is home.*

Sanaa Lathan is crying, an incessant wailing. And the child is crying too. A plea. A gasp, they are both out of sight, in the backroom, door shut, but it can be heard through the walls. Vonetta! calls her on her cell, and the crying stops.

There's a faint ringing, *hello*, she says, *baby girl, Lathan, what's going on*, Vonetta! says, *come from the back, come sit with me up front... what's the matter*; and Sanaa says *I can't take it.*

Take what, honey?
The child, Sanaa says.

Sanaa Lathan sits on the plastic couch. Her heavy head is on Vonetta's lap.

Net; she whines, nose running.

Hush, hush.

The pair is trying to distract themselves by watching Burle outside with the geese. Burle, laying in the snow, the snow in his mouth, in his nose, under his short fingernails. And we hear the child yelling, hollering, *mom, mom, mommy, mommyyyy, mom mom mommmm, ma, mom*; (anyway the woman doesn't care for the word, Mom, or any of the words that derive from 'mother': mōdor, mutter, moeder, mater, meter; mamma, material, matter).

What does anyone comprehend of the role? It's a thankless thing.

Mommy.

Net especially hates the letter *-y* at end, and any word that ends with the letter *-y,* and how people add the letter -*y* to words or names without permission, *Vonny!*, *Vonney!*, Burle sometimes shouts.

The plastic covering is sticking to Net, Netta, and the pink sling backs make her feel valued. The acrylic makes her feel done up.

The woman offers to watch the child for a while, her godchild, *just for a day or two. And the child can sleep over, just for the night, I can watch him.* What did she know about tending to a child? *Not much, not anything,* she tells us later.

Sanaa is beautiful, renewed, she takes out the flask, she eats pink peppercorns from the bag. We rub her back, we tell her, *get up, get up! Go out on the town.*

Lathan is up, she's out of it.

Lathan is standing at the window. Her skin with the large pores and the eyebrows plucked thin. A tiny little gap at the front, a barely visible gap, she eats a handful of almonds, almonds falling to the carpet.

Sanaa ignores the child, she can't respond to the cries straight away, *the child has to soothe itself,* she says suddenly, *they have to get it out of their system.* And even the way she says this too harsh thing is beautiful coming out of that gap in her mouth. *No, nope, no sir,* she says.

There are things to be sacrificed, you'll see Net, and turmoil will follow, she says.

The woman chomps down on the soil (acrid, chunky, and high in nitrogen).

You'll have to give it up, eating the dirt, sitting at the salt marsh, barefoot at all hours. Dirt all up under your fingernails, swallowing dirt, you'll see.

The woman pays hundreds of thousands of dollars a year for her nails to be prepared, designed, filed down into the shape of a coffin, and for the local flowers to be picked before the weather turns, and for everything to be preserved and installed onto her short nail beds.

The sweat is running down her chin and her neck. Down to her lower back. Sanaa Lathan does not seem to be sweating at all. The white refrigerator hums and the geese outside call out, like car horns beeping, or like a child's toy squeaking. Lira squeezing the life out of the toy, the toy is dead/dying, and Vonetta! has learned that some toys make sounds that can damage the ears of children, *the Hearing Associations says that a toy can make a sound as loud as 85 decibels and if held to the ear can be as loud as 100db, they say, '110db, or as loud as a chainsaw or a plane engine.'*

Oh, that navy man with so much time to waste watching animals in the snow. Burle.

What's the deal with him today?, Sanaa asks.

What's his deal? I don't know, he likes those animals, Vonetta! says. *He's always liked them... the wind with an average decibel of 30, a whisper too, and the birds at 122db, a baby's cry at 122db. The refrigerator (45db), don't they hum?*

All the surfaces are covered to preserve. Sanaa Lathan hangs her head out of the window, she yells. The man looks up. She waves her hand at him, bringing her hand away from her body and then close to it, her neck, her hand moving toward herself, fast, in and out, and then leaning on her suprasternal notch, *come*, she yells, *come over, come up!*

He stays where he is, in the snow.

Then he's up, wiping the back of his navy pants, wiping the elbows of his navy jacket, on his feet. He moves further away, behind an empty/bare willow tree and near a royal blue tent. We can't see any part of his head when he stands like that, only his arm and some navy material, his knees. *Mom.*

Sanaa Lathan moves from the window, she goes to the child.

The child stops with all the fussing when he hears the muffled footsteps approach on the red carpeting that covers the original hardwood, herringboned floors. The child settles.

Sanaa Lathan allows the mouth on her breast. Her breasts are not sticky with sweat, they hang just right and the milk is pulled out. Sanaa brings the child to the living room, past the kitchen with the humming refrigerator (50db), to the open window. She moves past the boxes, almost all of the belongings have been unpacked and placed back into their rightful place. There is only the lampshade to be returned, the paintings left to be hung.

The sucking is low (12db): [text that runs on the bottom of the screen.]

Vonetta! watches the child, the ravenous, *ravenous child,* she says.

Sanaa and the child move away from the window while Vonetta! looks for coins in the glass jar. With the child wrapped around the nipple and around the waist, Sanaa Lathan struggles to explain her troubles. She removes the child from her body and sets him down, just for a minute, to think, on the plastic. She tries to move quickly through her story, about the new man, Everton, how he is up under her like a child, and how she cannot, *I cannot handle a man that is like a child, and his eyes too, large and childlike, please*, she says.

Vonetta! sets the stool down in front of her, climbing, grabbing the glass jar from the high shelf, stepping back, pouring the contents out on the kitchen floor (27db). Sanaa latches the child back on. She bites the child's fingernails, down to the quick. She takes the tiny little hands into her mouth. She sucks the snot from the child's nose.

It's the simplest way to do it.

Lathan, the child says, creases lining the childlike forehead and the childlike neck—the proportions of which were formed inside of her.

A game token, a button, foreign bills, 1000 lire, and then the *.25, .50, .60, .70, .75, .90*, she counts. Mona's shit is in the jar, her little papers and mismatched pieces of jewelry, *look at her rocks and totems. The funds are low.*

The man is behind the willow tree. The woman doesn't feel like having company, *I'm glad Burle is hiding.* We rewind it to hear it again, *I'm glad, I'm glad.* Vonetta! is broke, in financial ruin, unemployed, desperate to sustain a lifestyle. Sanaa and the babe stand up and sit down, stand up, *is it a game?*, the woman says. They all return to the plastic couch. The child is latched on, he won't let go of Sanaa Lathan, or he cannot be separated from the source. He makes eye contact with the woman.

The fire truck moving past, speeding, a siren, *another fire then... and the honking of cars and the honking of geese for a moment combines to a total of 250db.* The open window with the sound of the high-schoolers again, and the heavy wind.

Forest green, the babe in his forest-green onesie, and the traffic lights in the street move every three minutes—yellow for three minutes, red for three, and three green minutes. People climbing over the asphalt to cross the street. The impatient bus driver, Charlie, honking like a maniac, and on the muted television (0db) the pair watch a repeat of *Living Single*. The child watching Maxine eat a sandwich with both hands, mouth open, delighted about something she knows but will not say.

The wall behind the white plastic couch is cold to the touch, a tremor from the elevator shaft going down, and the bass from the neighbor's stereo system. With her one humid palm she touches the child's feet, she warms them up; with the other she touches the wall, her pinky finger she touches Sanaa.

From next door, music (140db)—Nina's voice singing *nothing but feelings, c'mon clap dammit, what's wrong with y'all?* Nina's overbite coming down—the radio left on, the station, 98.7, still going on about the grace of God, *God's only begotten son*.

Upstairs the neighbors argue, a woman laughing and another one pleading, *at 150db and 170db respectively.*

This was a friendly building once, Vonetta! says, *remember?*

I was too young, no.

The neighbors were known, or they used to have some respect for one another, and remember how I used to teach y'all things: how to build a fire, how to quit a game, and later, how to quit a man. Remember? How they used to come, ravenous for advice or to remedy a thing. I used to say: 'cover up your body in witch hazel and vaseline, then swim out in the river, dive, touch the river floor, pick up a rock, bring it back, leave it at the door, go home, bathe, and go to sleep.' Then the lover will be sorry. Remember?

Only the arguing is known now. Everyone tends to stay to themselves, it's every man for themselves, Sanaa Lathan whispers into my ear. *Not many other things are shared or known.*

One of the new neighbors is named something that sounds like Clemmmme and we recognize the irregularity of Clemmmme's bowel movements, the toilet flushing at strange hours, or with long intervals in between, the woman says. *Feeeeelings,* Maxine's mouth, her gums.

The plastic and the guns, money or lack thereof, that's what the child babbles with the breast in his mouth.

We return to the man looking up, the man looking up.

The nerve of him!, and the decibels, what is the measurement?... *how he treats Mona, we have to talk about that. It's not right. And all Mona wants is some attention, damn. And how to measure sound most accurately?*, the child continues between gulps, *how?* There is a standard of measurement.

The sun, it shines, and does it not sound out? Is he coming?
Not this, not this, Sanaa says.

We're sinking—the humming fridge, yelling heard through walls. The mother's long nails. The child that is on the outside, how he slipped right out, Sanaa had hardly pushed. *We no longer kick. The sports team is practicing their kicking.* Lira smelling of soap and feeding; sinking. *A meeting from afar, or from a long distance; what is gathered only from a distance?*

Sanaa and the baby stand up to close the blinds, on their legs are the impressions left by the plastic coverings. Vonetta! stands up, the baby's hand is around her finger. Before they all touch the string, to the right and to the left, click, they see the man, Burle, he's looking up, looking right at them, it seems—at the breast, and at her ravenous child.

And the man seems apologetic, too, for having rejected their earlier invitation, or he seems to be interested in redefining something. He stands close to the willow tree, to the right of the willow tree and the snow-covered sidewalk, and the tents near the city hall, close to the geese and to the traffic. He is close to crying, and his face is fine. His navy elbows and his navy forearms, his navy skin and his eyes look fine, and his teeth, fine.

Mona enters, slamming the door behind her. Bam. She comes to the window. They stand in a straight line: The baby child, Lathan, Net, Mo. Beryl joining them from the kitchen, yes.

We make out his dark hair, twisted in geometric

patterns—like Iverson, braids tightened courtside, *Allen was born with the longest arms*, Ann, his mother, used to say.

Burle removes the durag to show them. For a second he lowers the material, he bows his head as if to say, '*see, see how neat and how fine? Vonetta!/Mona/Sanaa/Beryl/child/child?' Our child changes things, the child matters, he will come, Vonney, will he come? Can we begin?*

Then his scalp is covered up again; the two strings lapping around and around, tight against his forehead, wrapped flat and formed into a knot, with the synthetic cape moving behind him like an angel wing in a waterfowl.

SUPRASTERNAL NOTCH/88DB.

The man watches from below—surrounded by snow and the white-fronted geese—the six calling out to him.

PRICE OF ENTRY.

We've discussed the buildings before—are you sick of discussing them? The buildings are known, from the textbooks left behind, and in the libraries.

Whatever is left of the buildings and of the surrounding nature remain only because the community chooses it to be so. The topography remains. We see their effort, they commune and it's still Saturday, it's dusk, they have their Saturday meeting and their Saturday vote, and we don't mean to repeat it but the surrounding nature is key!

And what is the hierarchy of this space? Is it vegetal? Who controls public space?, Beryl asks.

The outsiders think in terms of capitalism, yes, of course, it is always at the center and it affects everything/everyone; but this place is guided more by emotion, the woman, Williams, says. *Funding as related to emotion, I can't stress this enough, and it can be seen in the direction of the programming. There is money enough for commercial building maintenance, but an extravagant budget was recently rejected in support of subsidizing housing. Big money is thrown into gerrymandering, dissappearings, or whatever things have become altogether criminal, bombings, craters in the earth, millions of dollars diverted from neon orange paint/botany! It is a wonder. We fundraise our own, funnel our own coins toward bags of ice, or a certain grade of paper, paper that is cut up and distributed for the purpose of the major Holiday (almost coming to an end).*

We are fuming, we place our vote. [*Outside a missile, or the birds, fireworks, a whistle moving up the scale,* Williams says. *A waterfowl dropping down/down, reaching the sidewalk under the ballot—a ruddy shelduck's demise is not unlike war.*]

The number runners collecting the bets on thick slips of paper, first thing in the morning. The tepid hot water bottle. The arm moves, the head follows. The wailing of a child. *All the children think they're grown?* The weatherman says *chance of rain*, we aren't convinced. The trouble runs so deep between us. The measurement of throats clearing. *This is moving slowly*, the narrator says. *Vonny*, she says. We put the pencils back on the desk. *But the movement has something to do with preservation, it is slow so as to not be lost. Isn't it enchanting to see those long friends close together, long, cold, the six horsemen, this bunch, limbs spread, a hand to the wound, a hand to the gut, the wide landscape in position behind?* [Someone offstage yelling, *hell no!*] This is correct, this pacing. *Come correct*, we hear the teens say. *Your head is in the gutter.* We are not clean with each other, we chassé to Feroza's, Sanaa buys us doubles with the tamarind sauce. Passed the geraniums, we arrive home (*home?*) and the neighbors are still at it. We set up the camera (*mother*) and the tripod, (*fucker.*) Later, when the tapes come out we are already gone, dust, *dead?*, and when they are distributed widely enough they will call it a mess, *a goddamn mess.*

CLAY.

Burle watches the women from outside, from downstairs and across the street. Mo, and Vonetta!, and Sanaa L., Beryl, little Lira. How they gossip! They all meet his eye. It's important to note, something imperceptible is shifting in him, a certain sense of freedom and detachment.

They have finished the deed, or they have all come to the end of something.

He brags to the neighbors. He takes credit for them, for bringing them together: *It's my voice that acquainted us all*, he says. *While I climbed across the asphalt, the way I would blow a tune, you know, I was singing about aching, about how my woman wasn't coming home, she's found a new man, lord knows that I've been trying, like Curtis Mayfield, or some shit like that, when I bust my ass. Was walking three steps behind, as is custom, fell, and all six of them women noticed me.*

All six women, they noticed me fallen, broken.

Now, Mo wasn't yet born, but Irene was pregnant with her. Irene was there by chance and Mona was kicking, she was there, and the others: Vonetta! Sanaa L., Seret, Beryl, Jackie— they were there. On the sidewalk the sound was soft, a raspy/ low fall.

The first one took me upstairs. A stranger, she took me. She bandaged me up and sat on my face to quiet me, to stop all my sad singing, and the second, Sanaa L., held my forehead with the heel of her hand, riding in reverse. The third one rolled the material down, away from her hips, away from the skin, she faked it, the fourth rubbed me down with witch hazel, the fifth took money from my wallet, and when I got up to leave them I tripped once more.

'Burle,' she said.

I caught myself against the dresser and there they were all five anxious, lost. It happened in the span of minutes: all that singing and hollering, pressing the button for the elevator, 16, someone mounting my face, my nose bent from the effort, and then how I got up, untangled myself from them, but went bumping into the dresser, into the piano stool. We rolled the material of the third one back up and around her hips. A clumsy man, they laughed. I thanked them, I said 'bye bye,' I left my number.

He enters the material in time with the song's humming. *Still tippin' on four fours*, working the clay, bending/rolling, wetting it, moving it. The pockets of its body are folded. He squeezes. He smoothes everything over, he presses with his fingers and pushes the petal with the ball of his foot. And now his elbow is upon it. His nose is upon it, an elbow upon a thing, the bags under his eyes, the hair follicles or something with hair.

He plays the numbers this morning, *4, 7, 9*. He moans, a thump.

He pretends to cry, he's moved by his task, completely overtaken by it, trying to complete the vase before the Holiday is up.

The man can be heard by the neighbors. Oh, the way he hums a song and the way he shows his elation at the arrival of this old task. *Back then hoes didn't want me*, the walls are paper thin. Floorboards are creaking and some of this place needs fixing. He hums. His studio set up in the abandoned first floor apartments. Water soaking his tennis shoes, his white socks.

And we know all about Burle's voice, its inflection and what it means for his voice to reach up high. *Something about creation*, the children say.

When the man is filmed exiting the studio, the neighbors look at him curiously. The neighbors are not surprised by his demeanor, or by his hair. They greet him—*hey Bur, a fine day, a fine day*—lines of burgundy on his forehead and on his arms the neon orange markings.

When he is done the man wanders, he goes about his business, to the barber shop or to grab some food, a meatloaf patty, or to bathe. The water running in the community center bathroom, cold: he washes himself clean.

Afterward, he takes a nap. And when he sleeps it is as if he is standing, standing tall like a boy is taught to stand tall, *stop with all that crying, stand up*—his posture is excellent (except for one shoulder that leans down a little) though he is exhausted, spent, sleeping.

Burle can be seen from the window, he's down there, and nothing of the lines on his arms or the marks from the clay can be seen. Nothing of the effort that has drawn him in, nothing of ceramics. He sleeps on the green bench.

The man is familiar, the neighbors know him, of course, when he stands on the street, one shoulder leaning, or when he sleeps on the bench near a tree that can be seen from the windows, and he sleeps in a way that is familiar. *And the married women know him, and the single men too*. All the women he has possessed and all the men he has seduced can be seen standing in their respective windows, watching the man—asleep.

When he wakes, hours later, still laid out on the bench, and on the last day of the major Holiday, he realizes how some people are, and that people aren't frank with themselves, not the way he is frank and honest with himself, *I'm a realist*, he says to us, to the camera.

Then he is gathering the green peas with his arthritic hands, shelling them, snapping. He sits outside to do it, two, three, four, five, twenty, one hundred individual peas, and the snap is loud. Three hundred peas? The bowl fills up.

SHOULDERS.

What these two sisters want is a mirror.

Yes, to see each other more clearly, or to run parallel.

See how the one follows the other? The one looking up to the other, an arm's length away? One has always repeated after the other, single file.

When one buys a cashmere thing, does the other not do the same? When the one changes the look of the cabinet, does not the other do the same?

Is it all too common a thing, for two women to share? For one to have had him decades ago, ages ago, and for the other to have him now?

I don't know—

It's too common a thing.

The woman has been with child for half a century, five decades, six, and it's quite boring for someone to be pregnant for so long.

Debilitating!

Burle is nothing to her, nothing to pine over.

Other fish in the sea!

The sisters are shoulder to shoulder, close, and full of umph...

The past is wretched.

And the two of them, these women, they want altogether different things.

No, it's only about this one thing, his shoulders, his shoulders and his goddamned silver cup.

LILIES TO SHREDS.

And the teenagers are sorry, *I am sorry,* the teen says, Seret says: *and we can be seen walking with heavy backpacks on, straps digging into our slight shoulders. Skirts rolled up, knee-high socks, sheer stockings. Uniforms. Someone calls out my name, 'Seret,' and I ignore it. The clothing is not comfortable. Everything is short, legs left out to dry. The school board wants us to be seen! Be visible,' they say. And they want the teens to be admired! And when the teens are admired it gives the administration a feeling close to triumph. It gives the school some funding.*

The teens are triumphant. We lean against cars. We scratch up the cars with keys and with the zippers from our jackets, coins. We unbutton our blouses. Thong straps pulled up almost to the waistline, gold jewelry layered all over and reaching down to our navels or covering our knuckles. Silver too. A petal, a pearl.

A lot of eye shadow and lip gloss, in nice tones, pink and orange and blue. Blossoming belly rings. What we carry weighs a ton.

Some days are better, and the rest are no good, no good, horrible days, emotions running high. Our best memories, when we look back upon this time will be a sound: plastic. From the open windows we hear it, all those who choose to cover a thing up, their furniture is preserved, oh, and how they wrestle around on it! Getting stuck to the plastic.

The teens collect plastic bags from the Chinese restaurant. Plastic forks and spoons. We use the plastic recovered from the streams to create our art projects. Or from the lake, the salt marsh. Plastic clips in our hair, plastic straws, microplastics sitting in the lining of our stomachs. Our hair: wrapped in a doobie, secured with hundreds of thousands of bobby pins.

Sometimes Juelz sits outside on Lenox, or on St. Nicholas

and we see him.

We laugh explosively/obnoxiously. (There are no two other words for the way teenagers laugh) and the way we torment anyone who shows their age is obscene. To wear your age on your face, or on your body, is akin to death. Aging is weakness, a failure, something to be avoided at all costs; foreign, an unfortunate happening that cannot befall us.

The teens are in the middle of it. That feeling. You remember the feeling? Some adults still know, they understand that feeling. Zoom in slow on our bright faces, dolly toward us. What beautiful skin! And we don't consider the lives of others, not enough or not at all, our guardians, our men.

We carry our lunches on the tops of our head, balancing bananas on our heads. Brains still growing. 'Fucking around,' Beryl says—long coats, navy coats, or a cropped jacket. Long nails made from powder, 3-D designs, acrylic on our toes. Algebra, that's what we're told we need to consider. Math, math! And sex. It goes without saying, the teens are made to obsess over it, to ponder its absence/abstinence, and therefore consider its inevitable sewing. The men waiting outside of the gate after school are prompt. They know how to erect a thing. There is that, and isn't it a gift for them to be so punctual?

The teens walk or they take the bus.

The women or the parents walking/climbing nearby, stroller, setting off across a street: the teenagers laugh at them. To be encumbered with another life is comical! Or we help reluctantly, the children climbing over to the other side. The teens ignore the flashing red traffic signs, completely/completely. We run into the road, the cars just missing us. ['Climb on sweetie pie,' the men call out. 'Bitch,' the men call out.]

Sometimes we climb up and on.

When we speak we use the language of place, it is entirely our own and all made up. We use the word 'long' to mean 'cold.' 'It is a long ass day,' we say. We use the word 'cold' to mean 'death,' 'dead.' We are free, too, to order our goddamn milkshakes (strawberry) and this freedom allows us to stammer, or to be taken at our word. We pretend all the time. To know things or not to know things. When we find something funny we laugh in a way that is explosive/obnoxious. Words: long, cold, innate, top.

The grown-ups remember that age: it is a sort of suspension in time, though they are suspicious of us; and for the most part there is lightness all over a young body. It is a desperate existence.

When teens pass the tents right near the city hall, they raise their voices an octave. We perform a cartwheel. 'Seret', they say, 'she is queer in her ways'. 'Seret, Seret.' 'She's decided to remain as she is! She doesn't want to move ahead,' and they are right. No one else has chosen this, to remain as is.

Everyday is about algebra; narcissism. For breakfast eating only a few things: bacon + egg + cheese (sharp cheddar) on a roll, cut in half, diagonally; or plain bagels w/a generous amount of cream cheese, toasted, well toasted, or honey barbecue chips, a quarter water, or even chicken broth with boiled vegetables and a drop of chimichurri sauce in the middle.

When the wind lifts up our skirts we scream. The strands of our hair shift over our noses like high grass, dyed in a green, dyed in a pink. Our little money goes to jeans, Jeans! To the Cool Grey's, to earrings. Money collected for playing with the ping-pong table at the arcade, air hockey tables. Laser tag, game tokens. In summer our skirts are wrapped around our waists, ballooning. Lapping at our waists like the Hutchinson, we move to bed. We ride the wooden rollercoasters. Do you feel that? Navy skirts draped over our foreheads, knee high boots, heads high, heels, and striped tights; the men reach, and if it's that time of the month we set a towel down on the edge of the mattress.

The moms are no longer allowed to touch our faces with a thumb, with saliva. The moon can no longer touch us. We're *spoiled rotten/spoiling. In the teens' estimation, everything is already ours. We believe that our parents' money, our guardians', our grandmama's, is also our money. The adults are ours to decide about. To ignore or to feel affection toward.*

We roll the skirt all the way up. We roll our eyes. Kiss our milky teeth. Skirts moving up the thigh, how they look at us! And the girls, only girls attend the all girls' high school. We put our hands on our knees, we wind up our little waists in the community center basement, dubbing, and we gather our knees to the chin when practicing, we sit with our legs crossed in the stairwell, inhaling. We let the men into our childish bedrooms or onto the plastic couch while our people are at work.

The reality is this—I remember playing with the hem of my mother's skirts. She wore skirts, yes, though there is nothing left of her to inherit. Did she exist? I do not know where she has gone to. A perfume, white musk, a necklace. A fire. I decided to stay the same, and I remain so. I was a teenager then and am a teenager now. I decided forty some odd years ago, fifty, that my life would be made right, low to the ground, young.

Did my mother unravel? A heart murmur, did it come? Living with them—with Mona, they are not my mother. Living with Jackie, Mona and the woman, Von, and sometimes with Sanaa, Beryl. A collective. Outside the poplar tree sways almost to the point of snapping. This godforsaken place is outside of my understanding. It is sinking. Can you feel that?

Too young for the cataract, though it blurs me up, the sky coming closer, everything becoming unrecognizable; though I understand the quiet of Mona's face and the exceptionality of Von's old face, a face I have known and known and known, since the beginning, moons ago—her mouth: a trumpet.

Sanaa's face I know, round, exquisite, gap in the middle. I understand the face of Billy Dee Williams in that film, stranded at sea, (stupid/pained/afraid). I have drowned him many a time, to save myself and to save the others. Billy Dee is stranded and did we have any other choice? 'Drive us,' she says. I know Mona's eyes, Von's eyes, Sanaa's wide set eyes, Pearl's eyes, Beryl, Beryl's eyes, Jackie's lower back, and at one time we all shared some similarities, in our mannerisms, or even the same mannerism, an adultish mannerism, our cycle.

Vonetta has skin like a curtain and a laugh that regales, or that regards. A face like Barbara O.; what else can be said—

We each bore a child, not Mona, but the rest of us, some stillborn, and the others play around our knees. They ask us for money. Didn't we sit in the inflatable pool and push a thing out? Quads. We drank a ton of water, pushed them out in water, in the living room of the apartment where we all reside. We had insisted upon it, performing this most natural thing in water, with the bottom half of us in water, we held hands, and those present said that the babies swam around with the umbilical cord still tethering them... the men waiting for us outside the school gate, they're real quiet/un-swimming...

(The tree is just about gone, the roots almost completely pulled out of the ground. It's hurricane season. The teenager's eyes are closed and their nostrils are open, and we cannot help but stare. The plastic making all that noise when we get up to leave, we're late, always late, and we push the couch up against the wall. And after we exit the front door, carrying the mangos under our arms, slamming the door hard, the men slip behind and follow us to the park. We don't return. The men speak to us, call out, whisper, not in a rough way, but soft, soft the way Sanaa is soft all over, up and down and around. And when we reach the swings, they come close. They push, we rise. Matches lets go of my hand to see about the whispering, she is spent, exhausted by the circumstances, and when she finds us again, legs swinging, wind at our backs, she places her hands around her mouth, hands like parentheses, mouth to our swinging ears, 'they want to crack us open,' she says.

I have drawn some eyebrows in with a brown pencil and I know how to fill the lips in with a brown pencil. The pencil as a tool, pencils sticking out of our hair, bite marks on our number 2 pencils, to doodle, to write down the goddamn solution. Sit in the green pencil case. Demerits. Detention. I'm late in the winter, long, ski masks and silver puffer jackets, winter tights. See our breath/we blow.

There is no more funding, no study abroad program. School is burned. The teens don't travel anywhere except around the Hill, really, and we smoke weed sitting on the blue mailboxes. The post office allows us. We carry the keys to our mothers' apartments, or to Mona's apartment, or Von's, Sanaa's, Jack, Beryl, Pearl, and we hold the tiny mailbox key in our pocket.

We sometimes break night. We sometimes seek shelter elsewhere, in a tent, or in the abode of someone recently married/ deceased, or we knock on the apartment doors of the neighbors, or we sleep in the community center basement. The water-damaged school. Have not yet turned off the hydrant, removed the hoses. A waterfall is coming out of the school, 'wow,' the men say.

The mothers of the teens roll their eyes when I come, when I ask politely, may I stay? And they say 'yes, yes, child, we have a spare toothbrush.' Or they kiss their teeth, and say 'goddamn' when they are forced to pull out the good sheets/towels/ washcloths.

The teens, we stare at our cellphones. We play hopscotch, double-dutch, and we are not double-handed. We practice these games, video games, mouth against a cartridge, blow a cartilage, a cigar. What we crave after school is chickpea soup, a salad made entirely of lemon; curry, coconut milk, roasted fennel.

What we get is a fry doused in ketchup and hot sauce: red/ yellow.

To walk to school—well, it was a dance. 2.7 miles. Between traffic, dodging bumpers. Unpaved sidewalks. No sidewalk.

Pushing the yellow tape on the back of the bus. Scotch tape sitting in a green pencil case, white-out, crushing pills, sniffing erasers, thumbtacks piercing through skin. Hoodies over button downs.

Jesus looks down at us from an angle—there is still Jesus in all of this, withstanding, youthful.

The school auditorium (burned to a crisp) is also the gym, also a screening room, theater/step club practice space/cafeteria. Vending machines used to click, tumble down. We tap our baby fingers against each other, picking flowers, leaves, tendrils. Crushing all the lilies to shreds.

KNEES.

We watch the footage, and we've been replaced. Sanaa Lathan is in it, but not us, not us. Sanaa is playing herself, no longer a documentary/document, we are gone: *removed, rejected/ejected*, we say. It is monologue heavy. Watching strangers, professionals, and our story is mixed up, and not right at all. *Summer sometimes changes to winter in ten minutes and a half,* Billy Dee Williams says in the third act, *while the knees of the woman bleed in the summer, scabbing. The weight of things bring her down, she goes down hard. Knees alive in winter, woolen. So affected by the ingenuity of shrubbery, the kick, by the geometry of a pile blooming/dying in a very determinate shape—an in-ground pool, wide feet. Moving in such a way that the knees buckle, give out completely, and if it's summer and the woman has on a short, breathable material her knees are left to die, or to line up for the gift—you're sweating,* the audience says—a dissolve, Sanaa Lathan, playing herself, daytime, downstage begins, interrupting—*the woman likes the shape of my knees, though they are not my favorite, not my cup of tea, and they're all banged up, from falling, bruising, skinning. I'm all scabbed up, scarred, when I look down at them, dry knees, there is always someone holding them apart.*

RUINSCHILD.

The earthquake was a 7.9 magnitude, it rung in the ears, and the sound carried down the street, the rumble like the blades of an overhead fan, *choppy waters, three people lost at sea*, down the hall the split was clean and decisive. The waters stood on its hind legs. Let's get through this then: *We ate dandelion greens, wild lettuce, leafy shit, and we never saw it coming.* The adults say, *get to the backroom!* We roll our eyes so far up, high, *Hosannah*.

And the woman, the old woman, the architect pretends to pick it up again, in the bed, in this soft grave of hers. *She is so curved, slow moving, slow going, kidney failing. Some of the lines of Lester Horton. Isn't she due? Horizontal swings, unmooring!*, the old woman covers her thighs with the long leather coat. *We can't think straight,* they say, *we are out of our depth.* The wind slices through our materials, still, we are leaning our weight, *the rotten bunch,* shifting around on our knees.

She stitched something into the skin, we realize, *something simple*, a running stitch on the old woman's forearm. Otherwise, she's used the pillowcase to form the creases, to mark up the body, right thigh, an indentation on her cheekbone. Marked with tattoos near the groin.

In our panic, we see the evidence of rural life—a paragraph on the exposed calf, and on the woman's wrists—*a landscape*.

And though we do not see it coming, (*the wave, the wave!*) the tending teenagers turn the woman's body over and over to see. They are rough with her.

They are rough with her, students, greedy, *mercy*, index finger pressed to skin, moving her limbs this way and that: beginning at the back of the neck, *what voracious readers*, and by the time they get to the old knees it is too late, shaking, finishing up at the sole of the foot, back to the lace of two wrists, using their index finger to follow the script of the horticulturalist:

> *the letters of an*
> *alphabet pressed from petals,*
> *stretch marks of an a b c,*
> *blind hem*
> *stitchings,*
> *or the old scars forced*
> *to call—*

PART IV, *the sound*

TAPE 1

After this sentence, the choreography begins,

Guava
Guava
Guava
Gu
Someone threw a guava at me. Fell on a schoolbus.
Buried Pig Roasted Underground.
Vongole.

—sucking our teeth, cohesively, slowly coming
to break you, off dried seed heads

and fingers elongating, perpetually pointed
get up out of bed, Jesus says, roll shoulders,
give neck...

in the hallway a relevé,
relating to soil
plots of vegetation, or the weight distribution
                                                    of the foot.

'Oh God.' The girls were moaning in chorus, grabbing arms
and jackets and pushing their backs against the shed's door
while lightning was panting somewhere on the far side
of the woods.

fan blowing, snap under some hiking boots.

my old man
tells me i'm
so full of sweet
pussy he can
smell me coming.
maybe
  i
  shd
  bottle
  it
      and
  sell it
  when he goes

voice 2 (quiet):

The center/roof among the vertical
tomatoes, the bird gourd,
primitive squats. Head between, and extended.
Keep your mouths shut: fed rehearsals,
counting
the Long Island Sound,

hinge down, right
a lateral T,
someone revving

voice 4 (low register):

Redwood grove and war
You and me talking Congo
gender grief and ash

I say, 'God! It's all so huge.'
You say, 'These sweet trees: This tree'

TAPE 2

voice (muffled):

or beginning with the wetlands
go undisturbed grey sediments
the waters stood on hind legs.
Hold some floods, the salt marsh trouble,
down the hall trouble breaking hips—
erosion, marine mollusks,
And the child?
Cordgrass (sometimes) reach 72 inches.

Straight up
and down and yellow.
Mussel songbird shorebird waterfowl
snow goose, enough shelter?
windblown soil transfers
spoil the shoreline

It is hazardous, blocking water access.

Sugar come / and sugar go / Sugar dumb / but sugar know
Ian' nothin' run me for my money
Nothin' sweet like winter honey

we
rode them, ate dandelion/lettuce.
Preserved all the way down, whatever, whatever
exists!, and oil to disinfect, clover

 [at our instruction, finally speaking into the mic.]

lilies erected, landscape urbanism
covers the left running stitch, dash
know about drainage

crease me, set these grasses then
against purple teasel, salvia, catmint, crocus, wisteria,
 buddleia, verbena rigida, lupine, morning glory, perennial wallflower, agapanthus, aster, aquilegia vulgaris, lobelia honeywort, honesty/lunaria, sea holly, grape hyacinth,
 passiflora, jacaranda mimosifolia,
russian sage, tatuaggio sul bacino, liriope muscari, globe thistle, globe artichoke...

(voice 2, movement):

Guess I better go ahead—see y'all later an tell you straighter.
You know if you pull out dem eye teeth you ruins yo' eye sight.
I God, you back here again.

thigh as rural life
they turn shape over like rotisserie
the bastards, begin back
neck, finish at the sole.

Oh! They act the sun.
They've been at it a while,
salt line on their shins
like a hem

suppose it was not here in the city but down on the beach
far into the woods and I wanted to go
there by myself thinking about God
or thinking about children or thinking—

TAPE 3

voice (no one/none):

you think the accident rate would lower subsequently

We could see what he meant
We could see it so clearly that we have made a list of our
own of things that are so daring—well...

spread a hand to wound
along the Hutch a cup / to womb
moving geraniums...

And I'm not done

I'm not about to blues my dues or beg...
...to fly slip slide flip run
fast as I need to
on one leg

We kept on, saying we were looking for our cowboy
and followed the day across the Pennsylvania green
until we left spring there in the high ground and the land
turned slowly grey and hard and cracking and we were
nearing New York State. The promised land.

voice (from the backroom the children's song):

What we found later
was the espionage.
Afternoons of spying.
Low-lying
socioeconomic
activity / salt marsh sediment
radiocarbon dating
casing, recognition land use
trend / core elemental isotopic
the pollen profile
RSL rise 32 percent
global average
thickest sequence peat / dent, coastal wetlands drain
fill along the Hutch, fail / chronology sedimentation
rate concentration
lead copper / isotope / highly drily
localized eventual
provenance / experiencing erosion
dancery
There is something federal going on,
playing all sides.
Playing the dozens,
She is sorry, in fact, so sorry.
We are intact, are we not?
So peel that man up from the sidewalk
His head split open like a melon!
Eat the seeds! Eat the seeds!
Teeth swinging, swinging red.
The other party is intact, are they not? The country?
We want to soften this earth
We want to soften this aftermath,
Hasn't she been the breadwinner?

*Lifting the breast
to get up under
with the wash rag, the bow frog,
and though we have lost some respect, we pine*

Notes

Several works in *PART I, the film:* include references to the Hill, a place among the works of August Wilson and Toni Cade Bambara. The phrase "the metal, metal, metal of waiting" occurs in a line from Dionne Brand's *Inventory*. "Look at the white shoes, look at the white shoes," spoken on the '90s television program *Martin*. "Obie, Obie" as a character/utterance borne from Toni Cade Bambara's *The Salt Eaters*. The hand of James Baldwin holding a cigarette, while speaking with Nikki Giovanni on WNET's *Soul!* (London, 1971), as collage, sitting above *Rock* by G. Ford. Ideas of lateness in architecture derive from *Lateness*, by Peter Eisenmen and Elisa Iturbe (2020). The communal film/social history set after Banu Cennetoğlu's 128 hours of footage.

In *PART II, the text:* a reference to landscape, the "dewdrop grass" and "no growth without decay" pulled from "Can Art Be Nature, Case Study #6 (Piet Oudolf)"; *Garden Futures: Designing With Nature*, Hanno Rauterberg, (2023). The inclusion/echo of songs "Didn't My Lord Deliver Daniel," from the *Book of American Negro Spirituals* (James Weldon Johnson, J. Rosamond Johnson, 1925); and "The Upper Way" by The Violinaires (1972). "The eyes are sympathetic," language taken from Alice Walker in the essay "Beauty: When the Other Dancer Is the Self" (1983). Returns to Diana Ross in *Mahogany,* the film by Berry Gordy (1975); Ross reciting "The world has not fucked me" on *The Russell Harty Show* (1975); "Diana Ross Live in Central Park" (1983/2012). The children singing a line from the Diana Ross song "Love Hangover" (1976), a line from "Lift Every Voice and Sing" (1900). Considerations of the 1997 film *Love Jones* by Theodore Witcher. A photo of Co-op City under construction from the International Ladies' Garment Workers' Union Archives, the Kheel Center, Cornell University.

From *PART III, the film continued:* a call to *Emotional Landscapes, on Burle Marx* by Jonás Romo (2018); stage banter by Nina Simone during a performance of "Feelings" at the 1976 Montreux Jazz Festival; the 2004 song "Still Tippin'" by Mike Jones; and a found image, *Untitled* (*Weems Wedding,* 1957).

In *PART IV, the sound:* suggestion of Derek Walcott's poem "Map of the New World," repeated mentions of the word "guava" from Jean-Michel Basquiat's untitled sketchbooks. The complete poem of "Homecoming" reproduced from Sonia Sanchez's *I've Been a Woman: New and Selected Poems,* thirty-three words from Toni Cade Bambara's *The Salt Eaters,* four lines from June Jordan's poem "For Alice Walker (a summertime tanka)." Language of Marc Santora's *New York Times* article "Scientists Glimpse New York's Perilous Path in an Ancient Patch of Marsh' (2017). Lines borrowed from *Mule Bone: A Comedy of Negro Life* by Zora Neale Hurston and Langston Hughes (1930). Four lines from June Jordan's "Poem about My Rights," one line from "Poem About Police Violence," five lines from "I guess it was my destiny to live so long" from *Directed by Desire* (2005). References to the article "Relative sea-level trends in New York City during the past 1500 years," from *The Holocene,* Andrew C Kemp, Troy D Hill, Christopher H Vane, Niamh Cahill, Philip M Orton, Stefan A Talke, Andrew C Parnell, Kelsey Sanborn, Ellen K Hartig (2017). A line reproduced from *Generations, A Memoir,* Lucille Clifton (1976).

Credits

Lucille Clifton, excerpt from "dialysis" from *Blessing the Boats: New and Selected Poems 1988-2000*. Copyright © 2000 by Lucille Clifton. Reprinted with the permission of The Permissions Company, LLC on behalf of BOA Editions Ltd., boaeditions.org. Lucille Clifton, excerpt from *Generations: A Memoir* from *Good Woman: Poems and a Memoir 1969-1980*. Copyright © 1976 by Lucille Clifton. Reprinted with the permission of The Permissions Company, LLC on behalf of BOA Editions Ltd., boaeditions.org. "Short poem" from the book *Homecoming* © 1969, by Sonia Sanchez, reprinted by permission of Third World Press Foundation., Chicago, Illinois. "For Alice Walker (a summertime tanka)", "Poem About My Rights", "Poem About Police Violence", "Winter Honey", and "I guess it was my destiny to live so long" from *Directed by Desire: The Complete Poems of June Jordan,* Copper Canyon Press © Christopher D. Meyer, 2007. Reprinted by permission of the Frances Goldin Literary Agency. Aerial view of Co-Op City under construction, August 4, 1970. Photograph by Thomas Airviews.

Every effort has been made to trace the copyright holders and obtain their permission for the use of copyrighted material. The publisher apologizes for any errors or omissions and would be grateful if notified of any corrections that should be incorporated in future reprints or editions of this book.

Fitzcarraldo Editions
133 Rye Lane
London, SE15 4ST
Great Britain

Copyright © Giada Scodellaro, 2026
Originally published in Great Britain
by Fitzcarraldo Editions in 2026

The right of Giada Scodellaro to be identified as the
author of this work has been asserted in accordance with
Section 77 of the Copyright, Designs and Patents Act 1988.

ISBN 978-1-80427-211-4

Design by Ray O'Meara
Typeset in Fitzcarraldo
Printed and bound by Pureprint

All rights reserved. No part of this publication may be reproduced,
stored in a retrieval system or transmitted in any form or
by any means, electronic, mechanical, photocopying,
recording or otherwise, without prior permission
in writing from Fitzcarraldo Editions.

Without in any way limiting the author's exclusive rights
under copyright, any use of this publication to 'train'
generative artificial intelligence (AI) technologies to
generate text is expressly prohibited. The author
reserves all rights to license uses of this work
for generative AI training and development
of machine learning language models.

fitzcarraldoeditions.com

Fitzcarraldo Editions

This book is printed with plant-based inks on materials
certified by the Forest Stewardship Council®. The FSC®
promotes an ecologically, socially and economically
responsible management of the world's forests.
This book has been printed without
the use of plastic-based coatings.

The authorized representative in the EEA
is eucomply OÜ, Pärnu mnt 139b-14,
11317 Tallinn, Estonia.
hello@eucompliancepartner.com
+337 576 90241